The Erotica Writer's Husband

& Other Stories

by Jennifer D. Munro

The stories in this book (some in different versions) have appeared in the following places, some under a pseudonym:

"Small Minded" as "Pinkie," ZYZZYVA, *Best of Best American Erotica 2008*

"Dicks, Digits, Dildos," *Best American Erotica 2004, Ripe Fruit: Well-Seasoned Erotica*

"Abstinence Makes the Heart Grow," *Mammoth Book of Best New Erotica V7, The Means*

"Fairy Tail," *Mammoth Book of Best New Erotica V6, Chiron Review*

"London Derrière," *Mammoth Book of Best New Erotica V3, Best Women's Erotica 2003*

"Dogs of Sayulita," *Literary Mama*

"Spat, Spud, Spatula, Stud," *Versal*

"Slake," *Mind Caviar, Penitalia*

"Pregnant Pause," *Shameless: Women's Intimate Erotica*

"Not Suitable for Children," *Kalliope Journal of Women's Literature and Art, Slow Trains, Clean Sheets*

"Doghouse," *Penitalia*

"Erotica Writer's Husband," *Mammoth Book of Best New Erotica V8, Best of Mammoth Book of Best Erotica 15th Anniv. Ed.*

Visit the author's website at *www.munrojd.com*.
Contact the author at *ginproductions@hotmail.com*.

en theos press
www.entheospress.com

ISBN-13: 978-1-105-60057-9

Second Edition

To the Erotica Writer's Husband,
for his gumption in the face of much misassumption.

Contents

Small Minded

*H*oly moly, what a penny whistle. I'm talking cherubic. I'm no size fanatic, but peckers like that should be attached to five-year-olds, not college graduates.

Tiny timber wasn't at all what I expected. This guy had a heavy-booted, open-kneed stride that warned of a boulder in the center lane. He walked through the bar like the fire hydrant anchoring his cul-de-sac might throw his hip sockets out of whack, an orthopedic nightmare. His pelvis thrust forward as he approached me, shoulders tipped back, as if to keep from toppling over from the staggering weight of the anvil crammed in his crotch. I was a drifting dock in want of a well-cast hawser, and he hooked his heel on my barstool. He offered me a Long Neck and a grin, and I needed no convincing to unleash the mastiff barking behind his fly.

Back at his tidy condo, he undressed without shame. Here he carried himself like he hefted Gulliver's package in the land of Lilliputians—but his cock rose up like a tender shoot in springtime.

Not that he'd tried to trick me with a zucchini stuffed down his jeans, but his attitude publicized a penis bigger than an asparagus tip. I'd dated tons of guys who'd measured their manhood, but this guy would have to go metric, using that centimeter side of the ruler I never bothered with. He had enormous hands and feet, too. Another urban myth shot to hell.

I should have known better when he introduced himself as Pinkie, but I figured he was nicknamed from his past as a sunburned Marine slinging a bazooka in the field. I learned he was never in the Service, that he had worked his way through school at a pencil factory. "Doing what?" I wanted to ask. "Posing for new models?"

The rest of him wasn't half bad. His abs rippled like they hoisted old-growth lumber, not a sapling. His gluts were mountains of muscle to counter-balance a nether load. His biceps bulged as if he'd curled the orca in his pants since puberty. And his face radiated sincerity. Nice. Chiseled in the way his alabaster pilaster wasn't. He reminded me of those magnificent castrated statues. I always stare at the part I'm supposed to ignore. Except Pinkie could stand un-fig-leafed in the Vatican, and no one would notice.

I was aware of my hypocrisy even as I dried up in the face of this letdown. I was no better than a zit-faced teenage boy sniggering at small tits, worse than Joe Mechanic slobbering on his Muff-ler wall calendar while he scratched his sagging butt. I was measuring Pinkie by external standards he couldn't help. A diet or exercise regimen couldn't fix his little shortcoming. But *still*. A girl can't help but want a sausage with the works when she's hungry, not just a baby dill. They say it's the motion of the ocean that matters, not

2

the size of the boat—but I required a seaworthy vessel, not a toy submarine.

"Don't worry," he said, noticing my concerned stare once he'd slung his 501s aside. "I know what to do with it."

He rummaged in his dresser drawer, I imagined for a condom. Did they make them that small? I worried the sheath might slip off, like a kid's foot in a grownup's shoe.

Maybe the sprout would magically blossom once aroused. Penises can surprise you that way, a nifty trick compared to the inner mysteries of a vagina. So when he stepped next to where I lay on the bed, I swizzled it around on my tongue like my piña colada straw. Alas, the wee widget was hard already.

He got into bed with me. Pinkie was a nice kisser, with a shaved face and brushed teeth. I could tell by his moans and his arching against me that he was turned on. But not much else gave me a clue, though we were tight linked. I suppose this is what straight men feel, having to guess their lover's inside temperature with no barometer hung outside the house.

"Is it in?" I asked. I wasn't usually this passive in the sack, but his little stump stumped me. His tool rendered the girth-length question irrelevant, because his lusty laddie had neither. Forget the G-spot debate—if I had one, he'd never reach it.

"Oh, um, I haven't started." He tucked my hair behind my ear. "Don't you like foreplay?"

A further predicament between his legs distracted me—the boy had full, bull ballocks, perhaps the reason for his deceptive, Percheron-straddling stance. The swollen, twin soldiers dwarfed their commander, like Titan and Goliath flanking a shrunken Napoleon. They strained at the injustice of a midget firing off their potent ammunition. I feared sudden movement might snap the fragile twig wedged between two cannon balls. Talk about a turnoff.

Pinkie cuddled up with me. "You know the Greeks considered small dicks beautiful. Like us today and big boobs. Check out their painted urns. Hercules had a teeny weeny."

The Greeks also killed Socrates. But you had to admire a guy who said "weeny" with a straight face.

"They thought it meant better fertility," Pinkie continued. "Like today guys with low counts in their baby batter have to wear boxers—less heat to kill off the little tadpoles."

"So the Greek race might've died off in tighty-whities, huh? Togas saved democracy."

Pinkie's eyebrow shot up, a gesture that slays me for my inability to master it. "I pegged you for having more imagination than this, Giselle."

"You did?" Nail in the guilt coffin—he remembered my name. I'd wanted to get in his pants fast, so introductions had been hasty. I'd anticipated stanchion, not chopstick, not guessing that small talk would be more satisfying than floundering around with a small wick for a big candle.

"Sure. Your outfit's funky. I could tell you didn't just buy it like that. You did stuff to it. Made it you."

The universe was so unfair. The only straight guy on the planet who appreciated a strategically-placed appliqué had an insufficient needle for my basting.

"I'm sorry Pinkie. I mean, this is nice and all, you're sweet, but I didn't exactly go on a pub crawl tonight looking for sensitive husband material. If you know what I mean."

"No. Tell me. Now come on. Don't clam up on me."

Poor choice of words, considering my faltering libido.

"You girls always complain that guys won't talk, but getting you to tell me what you want's like pulling teeth."

I could see the dilemma of his previous lovers, disinclined to engage in an honest heart-to-heart. *Well, Pink, I want a Big Dick, massive fireworks in my mailbox, dynamite and bottle rockets, and you've got a sparkler, honey. Gimme Boom. Not tthhpphhtt. Glad we talked.*

"Come on, Giselle. Your wish is my command."

Right. His magic wand didn't look capable of miracles. A piccolo player couldn't orchestrate rough and tumble hockey sex, no matter how clearly I enunciated the choreography of my desires.

"Okay, maybe you'll do better with multiple choice." He pulled out the dresser drawer he'd been fishing in and dumped its contents on the bed.

Never having defended his country, Pinkie had quite the arsenal. He displayed Santa's Little Helpers one by one. "You prefer matte or glossy? Neon or *au naturale*? Animal-shaped or lifelike? Motorized or manual?"

Pinkie did the impossible and rendered me speechless. "You pick," I managed.

"You I can't peg. You're fun." He held up a psychedelic bunny, whose nose twitched at the touch of a button. He twitched his own,

5

and I laughed. "But also down to earth." He held up a flesh-colored, veined penis so realistic as to be disturbing, as if it had been lopped off a buckskin horse. It seemed lost without a body, reaching for contact like a blind man's hand.

"I guess we'll just have to try them all," I said sadly.

"That's why I couldn't guess! See, I knew you were different. Lots of girls won't use stuff like this. Think they're dirty or something. They get embarrassed. But not you."

He displayed various harnesses: thigh, pelvic, unflattering briefs with strategic holes. "But other girls tell me their boyfriends won't use toys even when they ask. The dudes feel threatened or something. Like their cocks have to do the whole job or they're failures."

"And you don't mind?"

"I'm sleeping with other guys' hard-up girlfriends, aren't I? What's to mind about that?"

I touched his wrist. "I don't know how to ask this without hurting your feelings."

"You hardly mince words, Giselle, and I like that. Don't start now."

"How do you manage to have such a positive attitude about, you know. Seems like other guys with, you know, might grow up to be angry women-haters, for getting laughed at or rejected. Or at least they'd be embarrassed about it. Not so open."

"That's the thing. Women never made fun of me. They felt sorry for me, which was worse. So I set out to prove them wrong. That I didn't need their pity. That *they* needed *me*. I did my homework. Mama taught me you could learn anything from a book, and she was right."

"A librarian's wet dream." Suddenly I was happy to be listening instead of lusting. Pinkie's voice filled me up the way his mini-macaroni might not.

"Mostly I read fashion magazines at the checkout stand. I couldn't believe what they sneak in after the makeup columns. Guys should beat off to *Cosmo*, not skin mags. Plus I learned that stuff like trimmed toenails matters to girls."

"The things they should teach boys in sex ed."

"It's the guys who laughed at me. I took heat in the locker room. That's the only reason I knew something about me wasn't right. So I lifted weights. Beat crying over it. Then I beat the crap out of the bastards if they gave me a hard time." He laughed. "Assholes. I can't believe the way I see dudes treat girls. So maybe my, you know, is the best thing that ever happened to me, so I don't turn into a jerk. And as far as I can tell, I'm getting way more action than they are." He held up a Hello Kitty vibrator and winked. "Time to tame the wildcat."

"*Mmrrooww.*"

Having the genuine article inside me after a parade of stimulating impostors ended up being more fulfilling than I expected. It wasn't the motion of the ocean that mattered, but the moving of Pinkie's heart. After I married him, turned out the Greeks were right. His baby batter worked just fine. It's too early to tell whether our son inherited Pinkie's signature centerpiece, but with a father like his, either way he'll do just fine.

7

Dicks, Digits, Dildos

*P*enises. Vibrators, dildos, tongues, even pens in my hungry youth. Fingers—mine, men's, rubber-gloved doctors', and one fumbling young girl's before boys occurred to me. Spermicides, sponges, diaphragms, condoms, lubricants. Seven-day yeast infection treatments—they didn't used to have the quick and tidy fixes they do now. Acidophilus tablets, vinegar douches, progesterone creams. Chocolate syrup. Tampons I could never tolerate—they just never felt as good as on those horseback-riding ads. Two miscarriages. Thermometers when we were still trying for kids. A quack regime of herbal vagi-packs during my holistic phase. Four-hundred ninety-two periods. Sixty-seven speculums. Forty-three pap smears. One cryosurgery. One hysterosalpingogram, as difficult to tolerate as it is to pronounce. Two biopsies. Eleven ultrasound wands. And this particular cock, my husband's, 4,682 times. I'm sure I've left some things out. At my age I have a hard time keeping track of what's trespassed between my legs.

Shouldn't all this have earned me some loyalty? After seeing it through so much—the ups and downs of a lifetime, so to speak—my vagina picks a hell of a time to betray me. It's our thirty-first wedding anniversary. And we've never had an anniversary without nooky. But I'm dry as a dead insect stuck in the lampshade. Parking lot closed for business, neon sign flashing, parking arm down, tires will be slashed if you enter the wrong way.

There I am, spread-legged while my husband hunts around in his softening state like a worm lost at the edge of a leaf. Not that he was rock-hard to begin with. Instantaneous erections happen only in the mornings, now.

Never mind the lubricant. I feel fragile, that I will rip and tear if he succeeds in his coaxing entry—like my grandmother's transparent skin, bruised by a whispered touch. Even my husband's soft cock feels angry against my desert tenderness.

You'd think there would be nothing left to shame me. This man has seen my flesh jiggle in every possible sexual position over the course of thirty years. I'm twenty pounds heavier than on our wedding day, when I foolishly starved myself into a dress I couldn't fit into two days later. Once, in the emergency room, he stood behind the doctor as the speculum was tightened. "The cervix," the doctor announced with a flourish of his gloved hand, as if he had created its hidden wink. "Wow," was all my husband said.

I have been inadequate in producing the requisite children. Deficient in jeans size, cooking skills, apologies, and in-law relations. I got over all that and concentrated on blow jobs and yoga stretches instead. You think my husband minded unmatched towel sets and my shopping without coupons?

But feeling sexually inadequate after all these years, when the lack of children gave us space for sexuality that so many couples don't have? When is my body going to cut me a break?

Fourteen years ago, reaching for the box of tissues to wipe up (he, always solicitous, tucks a tissue between my legs before he tends to himself), our hearts still pounding, my husband looked at the clock. "It takes us half an hour now. Used to be twelve minutes." Oh, we laughed at that one. But there's nothing funny about not being able to do *it* at all.

My vagina is a hand-puppet with nothing to say. I am the mouth of a rolled-up sock, crusty and used, discovered with mothballs under the bed. No O'Keefe flower, but a cracked lobster claw. The Star Trek alert sirens go off all around us: *Frigid vagina alert! Menopause approaching at warp speed!* I beam myself out of the room, after first meditating on dinner choices and considering the feng shui ramifications of our bed placement and wall color. Intense concentration has earned me many orgasms in the past, but I don't want to think about what's happening down there, my husband the spelunker rooting around for the opening of a collapsed cave. Think I'll get him one of those head lamps for Christmas. At the moment I wish ole Columbus would give up, abandon the exploration as a lost cause so I can return to my flower bulbs.

He knows I've vacated the continent. I've got the same look as the one I wear when I'm naked on the scale. As on the first day of my period, when I don't want him to watch me dress, feeling like

10

I've tripled in body size. Not a hostile look, like when he crawls into bed with cigar farts or enters halfway through a five-hankie TV movie and snorts at the obvious stupidity of the characters. It's the "Stay Off My Planet" look.

"Never mind," he says, rolling off me. "I have an idea. Something new."

After one-third of a century together, what else can be tried? Creative positions have gotten trickier with the need for glucosamine supplements. I could tell you what we've done on every stick of furniture in the house, but lately we stick to the basic bedroom standbys.

He fumbles around in the special dresser drawer, his thwarted pecker dangling below his belly flab. I admire his ease. Orgasms never elude him. Unexpectedly flaccid states don't disturb him. His confidence remains firmly rooted in his slightly above-average cock size (he's measured), and nothing seems to shake it. Not weight gain, hair loss, or below-average height. Even when he wore a dress a couple of times, his penis was *present* in his attitude. He never tires of me watching him, no matter which end of a diet he's on.

But now he turns away from me. His bum never changes no matter how the rest of him morphs over the years. "I got us a present," he says.

This current dilemma hasn't blindsided us out of the blue. My body's been working its way up to emergency drought levels for months, but I've ignored the signals and haven't practiced water rationing. I have procrastinated the doctor's visit, dreading the prognosis and resultant pills—but it now appears that *he's* been taking some preventative measures.

"I thought we said no presents this year." After three decades together, we buy for ourselves when the mood suits us. No more dropping months-long hints that the other one never gets.

"No, *you* said no presents this year."

There is a great deal of rustling going on. He's dropped down to the floor, so I can't see him over the side of the bed. I even hear him giggle. A fifty-four-year-old man, giggling! I giggle in response. We're a pair that way, like pizza and acid reflux.

He stands and faces me. "Tah dah!"

He has strapped a miniature dildo to his leg. A little Bacchus sprouting from Zeus's thigh. It is lifelike in shape and color, as if his cock has reproduced, a tiny silicone replica of the real thing.

He climbs onto the bed next to me. "Come on. There's more holes here than just one."

"You're gonna fuck my ear?" Fifties kids, we still love the thrill of foul language. Not during sex, but as part of our banter. "Wanna fuck?" we say. Or, with his Midwestern lack of verbs, "I need fucked."

"No. Your nostril. Now open wide."

I flare my nostrils, one of the few small muscle movements I can manage. He can wiggle his nose like a rabbit, but when I try it, my whole face contorts.

He wags Bacchus in my face. I swat him away, laughing.

I know what his intentions are. And he's incorrect. This isn't something new. Although I rarely let a chance go by to point out that he's wrong, since it's maddeningly infrequent, I keep my mouth shut. But we *have* tried anal sex before. Years ago. Before the twelve-minute era came to an end. We tried it only once, just for kicks during my Dickens phase, when I learned that at that time anal sex was the preferred method of "birth control." The literary experiment didn't work out, and we never attempted the back door method again. I never saw the need while my other hole was cooperating.

He lies beside me, his hand on my chest. My breasts have always fit perfectly into his palms. "I got a really small one, just for you," he says. "I remember that the last time it hurt."

So, he *does* remember.

"Come on." He nudges me to roll over. I sigh and roll my eyes, but comply. He rubs oil between his hands and massages my back. He sits back on his haunches, and Bacchus tickles my left buttock.

"Watch the armpits!" You'd think after spending more than half a life with me he'd have memorized the ticklish spots, which encompass most of my body, and tread a fine line with my erogenous zones.

"Yeah, dummy," Bacchus pipes up in a high-pitched nasal tone. Inanimate objects in our house have developed voices over the years, usually in falsetto, facilitating our highly evolved and effective means of dysfunctional communication. It is best during arguments to have a third party to blame, especially when the object has no vocal cords and cannot defend itself. We attribute the long-term success of our marriage to this system, though the African violet resents taking the heat for eating the last cookie, or for certain foul odors permeating the room.

"Sorry."

He skims his hands up and down my spine, across my tush. I begin to relax. I'm warm and expansive. I am an O'Keefe blossom under the New Mexico sun, splashed on the bed in purple and pink hues.

He spreads me, and I let him. I know that my ripe and rippled derriére will never make a magazine photo spread, but I also know that these cheeks look good to him. He slips inside, a centimeter at a time. It's not difficult at all this time, like the last time we tried it in the prehistoric age of our careless youth. Maybe it's because of Bacchus's minute size, or the lubricant, or our ability to work together, or that my lifelong lover has learned patience and self-denial. Whatever the reasons, I moan. I let him enjoy pleasuring me while he receives no physical gratification in return, only the sensation of giving. His real cock dangles and knocks against my lower back as he moves, right above my birthmark. His leg hair prickles my bum.

He can't tell what my vadge is up to, but I'm well aware of the state of his cock. It rapidly returns to its instant fossilized state of youth. He stabs my birthmark now with each gentle thrust inside me. My vagina stretches, yawns, and blinks, discovering that her coveted spot in the hierarchy has been usurped. Worse, the instigator is not even a member of the immediate household, but a Lilliputian godhead. Jealous, she puts up a fuss, causing a commotion between my legs. She even resorts to calling in the reserves, and my clitoris joins the clamor.

"I think Bacchus needs some air," I say over my shoulder.

My husband—this lifelong friend and lover who knows me better than anyone and yet doesn't know me at all—rolls off and lies beside me. He gazes at me, not expecting anything, though his Big and Little Dippers demand otherwise. He plays with my hair. For years he looked forward to its turning gray, saying with a wink that he wanted to sleep with an older woman. I know that in his rich inner life I've often been the siren schoolmarm seducing his helpless virginity, so I've never wrestled with hair dyes, despite the random streaks through the still-shiny black.

Then I'm on top of him, our puzzle pieces connect, and my body swallows him in one easy gulp.

Bacchus taps my rump, as if to say, *Hey, did you forget about me?* But he doesn't say a word.

Abstinence Makes the Heart Grow

"Pelvic rest," Dr. Frank prescribes. Dr. Frank is anything but frank. Despite a career based on the consequences of coitus, the obstetrician rarely mentions the carnal act that lands Lucy in stirrups. As if he can hide what his probing fingers are up to, he rearranges the drape between Lucy's spread knees every time she swats the paper sheet down. He unscrews his medieval instrument and snaps off his lubed latex glove. Rushing off to palpate his next patient, he leaves his assistant to translate the euphemistic instructions to Lucy.

"Pelvic rest," the nurse murmurs, handing Lucy a box of tissues. "No lifting, no intercourse, no exercise." She sandwiches the allusion to naked, intertwined limbs between two acts suitable for teatime small talk, sneaking in the indelicacy like unsuccessfully disguised vegetables in her children's dinner.

"No sex?" Lucy clamps the tissue between her legs. "You're *kidding*."

"Most women would be grateful," the nurse clucks. "Especially in your condition."

Dr. Frank advises physical restraint because he can do little else other than monitor the baby's progress. Despite a barrage of tests, he can't diagnose the reason for Lucy's previous miscarriages. So he errs on the side of caution, recommending that she not rock the baby's boat. Although most expecting women can boff with abandon in between barfing and bathroom visits, refraining is advisable with Lucy's unfortunate history of early pregnancy losses. She agrees without legal counsel to everything he demands of her. As if she was in any position to argue, spread like a poked bug on the exam table.

Raised in the post-feminist era, Lucy had believed that her body was her own to operate as she saw fit. But Dr. Frank orders the protection of Lucy's vaginal domain like her father issuing curfew twenty years ago, hitting her with the sledgehammer realization that emancipation was a deception. Once this miniature guppy takes up residence inside her, her pussy plays second fiddle. She no longer conducts desire's melody. Ian's staccato, long-tailed musicians can swarm her orchestra pit no more. One of the little buggers hit the right note and did the trick, and now her musical score shows only silence: a pelvic Rest mark stretching on for months.

Lucy resolves to make whatever sacrifices the butterfly heartbeat inside her requires. After all, her mommy friends complain that new parents surrender a great deal, including frequent and spontaneous sex, and none of them seem to mind. Now that Lucy's about to enter the holy ranks of motherhood, she determines to go cold turkey on profane language and lusty acts. But, once denied her, shtupping is all Lucy thinks about.

Lucy doesn't expect turning off the fucking faucet to be difficult, especially given her protective concern over the fluttering life inside her. Taken off guard by the unexpected medical instructions, she doesn't comprehend its ramifications until she goes home with her new living luggage and forces herself to ignore the waves of desire washing over her. If only she'd seen abstinence coming down the pike, she and Ian would have crash studied the Kama Sutra the night before instead of having a lukewarm quickie.

"Pelvic rest. Doctor's orders," Lucy informs Ian that night as he reaches for her boob. Her chest's transformation from pubescent to sex goddess proportions not only amazes and arouses them, but also awes them as the only wondrous visible sign of her three-month pregnancy. She backs away from him for the first time since they fought over Lucy's impetuous desire for a Chihuahua months ago.

"What's that mean?"

"No sex."

"Like, no coming, or, you know, like, no, um, the whole nine yards?" Like the doctor, Ian stumbles over precise terminology.

Lucy hadn't considered the various interpretations of the doctor's restriction. Ian thinks *"pelvic rest"* means no sexual intercourse, specifically, Ian keeping his perpetrating penis out of Lucy's vulnerable vagina. "Think of all the activity. It can't be good." He thrusts his hips to illustrate his point. He doesn't think "no sex" excludes sixty-nines. But Lucy believes that orgasm must be the dangerous part of the sex equation, because of the powerful contractions of the uterus.

"Well, okay, no sex, of any kind, period," Ian shrugs. "Whatever you think is best." Ian gives up pawing her body too easily for Lucy's liking. Shouldn't he look more wounded, like any romance hero would when his damsel rejects his passionate kiss because of nefarious secrets?

"What do you mean, it's '*okay*'?" Lucy cries. "It's not *okay*. You can give it up, just like *that*?"

"No, yes, I mean—Christ, look, what do you want me to say?" Ian rolls his eyes, a genetic behavioral predisposition Lucy hopes the baby will not inherit, although she prays the baby will be blessed with Ian's swift metabolism. "It *has* to be okay, right?" Ian folds her into a hug. "We'll get through this. We're having a *baby*." He squeezes her, hard. He squeezes the concern right out of her, deflating her irritation, and she knows everything will be all right despite the tiny pink judge between her thighs pounding her pearly-gavel and shouting, "Overruled!" Lucy's body is no longer a democracy of desire. The baby reigns as supreme dictator.

Lucy is too mortified to call the doctor's office for a more explicit definition of "*pelvic rest*," as if she might give away the secret that she and Ian had copulated for more than the utilitarian purpose of replicating their gene pool. Lucy refrains from any suspect activity. She wants this baby above all else, and surely can handle carnal deprivation for a few months.

The pregnancy books taunt her, painting gleeful images of pregnant women who experience their first orgasms, most powerful orgasms, or first multiple orgasms once they're knocked up. With the "engorgement of genitals" (now there's a sexy term, Lucy thinks) caused by increased blood flow to the pelvic area, sexual response can be heightened. Lucy doesn't inform Ian that the tight fit may also increase the man's pleasure—better that he not know what he's missing. Lucy herself has never come twice. She rips the page out of the book and burns it.

She successfully ignores her bloated labia, but her swollen breasts torment her. She's gone from a buoyant B to a dense C cup. Rolling over in bed is sensual torture, as her mammary glands bump into her arms, the pillow, and Ian's side (how can he sleep so deeply with all this deprivation going on?). With one whispered touch, her boobs instantaneously communicate their demands via live wires to her clitoris. She cups her full and hefty breasts in wonder—they now overflow her small palms. Her hands pluck constantly at her underwires to give her enormous areolas room to breathe. Her knockers feel as noticeable as semi-truck headlights. And they're tender. One lick from her husband's expert tongue and she'd traverse interstellar erotic realms, transported by haywire hormonal wiring. It makes no sense to her. Once pregnancy is achieved, shouldn't nature tranquilize the clitoris? There's no evolutionary purpose in her yoni's incessant yammering. She surmises that maybe the body craves ample sex in early pregnancy in order to store pleasure before starvation, like Joseph and the grain, predicting sexual drought once the baby arrives.

Ian sometimes forgets the ban and cups her breasts. Their ardor increases at warp speed when they touch, their skin sizzles, but passion is now as forbidden as the early days of their romance when there was no safe place to do the nasty, not in the twin bed she'd grown up in or in his barracks' bunk. She pushes him away. Her breasts are a loaded camel marching across the desert tundra of her deprived body.

Nothing about Lucy's body signals her to knock off the screwing. Her amorousness increases rather than slackens. She hasn't had a single morning of nausea. To the contrary, she feels bountiful and ripe for the plucking. Her body wants the sexual congress to stay in session, before she grows as big as a house and Ian's cock can't reach her front door. She can hardly bear to give Ian a goodbye peck, she stands so close to the unforgivable gulf of temptation. She hovers on the precipice of sneaking in a quickie, but it's not like cheating on a diet, when one cookie can't hurt. If it weren't for the doctor's order, she wouldn't be able to keep her hands off herself.

Mundane events provoke her ardor. The almost undetectable vibration of water rushing through the garden hose sends her into a paroxysm of desire. Kneading bread dough reminds her of squeezing Ian's ass. "*Rear end*," Lucy mentally corrects herself. And forget the electric toothbrush—she switches to a manual Harry Potter brush so that she won't try anything under his watchful gaze. The blender, hair dryer, and battery-powered razor are all banned for the current they transmit to her clitoris.

To give an extra nourishing boost to the fetus, she navigates progesterone suppositories up her twat twice a day, careful not to brush surrounding erogenous zones. Dr. Frank's pharmaceutical prescription further aggravates her rabid lust, as if he and God are in on a cruel plot to test her forbearance, like giving Job a raging hard-on in addition to his other trials. At first Ian dispensed the pink pussy pills, on the excuse that his long fingers could push them closer to the baby, but Lucy put a stop to his lingering ministrations. Her vagina went into eager spasms at his probing hands, like a piranha sensing the proximity of fresh meat. She administers the bullet-shaped, waxy pills quickly while visualizing explicitly unerotic images such as St. Bernards drooling or her cat's hairballs. But the instant she lies on the bed, her hands prying between her naked thighs, obscene images plague her: naked rock stars kidnapped and bound so that she can ride their pylon cocks; rolling with dark and tortured poets in the crashing surf; frontal and rear views of Antonio Banderas riding horseback nude while calling her name in his irresistible accent; and Ian on a long afternoon in bed with Belgian chocolate and an ice cold bottle of Veuve Clicquot champagne—Ian who knows exactly how to use his fingers or tongue or body to bring her to climax even on difficult days when she thinks she can't, when she's too overwhelmed with mundane distractions. He knows how to divert her attention to matters at hand, how to summon her mind to the core of herself that nestles between her legs—*ohh!* Lucy jumps out of bed, clinical hands smelling of her sex clamped in her armpit, and she furiously scours the toilet in order to redirect her unmatronly thoughts. She will *not* fuck this up. *Mess* it up, Lucy corrects herself.

Between her own fingers, the speculum, the doctor's gloved hands, test swabs, and the ultrasound wand, about the only thing that never sees the inside of Lucy's vagina is Ian's cock, the object that got them into this predicament in the first place. Lucy craves the intimacy of joined bodies, the return of the love act that unifies them each night after the long days in which their opposite personalities and habits drive them apart. He suggests that a blow job might not be against doctor's orders. The union would be a physical bonding of some sort, at least. But Lucy can't step down that dangerous road. She could not restrain herself from culminating the desire such an act would arouse. She would slip down the carnal crevasse as surely as a climber scaling Everest in bowling shoes. She calls Ian a typical male for his request. She can't stand herself.

"Sophia Loren went to bed," her mother tells her, "and she finally had a baby." If luscious, fertile-looking sex symbols like Loren and Marilyn Monroe had trouble maintaining a pregnancy, unremarkable Lucy doesn't think she stands a chance. Christ, their boobs were child-bearing billboards. Talk about Mother Nature practicing false advertising. Not being stacked, Lucy stacks the odds in her favor and goes to bed. Permanently. Although inactivity will hopefully improve the baby's chances, total bed rest also allows her to cave in to her growing depression. She worries that she's not fit for motherhood. What kind of sexual monster is she? What is wrong with her that makes her so goddamned painfully horny all the time? Maybe she is an undiagnosed nymphomaniac? Waves of peace and joy over impending motherhood battle breakers of resentful lust inside her, her Christmas-mind duking it out with her WWF groin. Maybe if she ceases to interact with the world, she can lure her mind out of the gutter. Even the bus driver in his brown polyester uniform looks hot to her. But going horizontal only gives her more time to fixate on not fucking.

She banishes Ian to the hard and lumpy couch because she can't stand the close proximity of his penis, which yearns towards her and stabs her under the sheets. She accuses his cock of communicating in sign language to her clitoris while they sleep. By all telltale signs his pecker is having as much of a problem forgetting its nerve endings as her pussy. His bulging basket knocks against her when they snuggle, like an insistent homing pigeon banging on her closed roost.

Lucy takes an extended absence from her job and rents a stack of subtitled foreign movies in order to dull her lascivious mind, but accidentally brings home a scorching Hispanic film. Raw sex scenes open and close abundant and explicit fucking throughout the story—she can't turn it off—and blister her thighs from the television screen across the room. Her clitoris doesn't need to read the captions to get the gist. Lucy sleeps with her hands pinned under her pillow so that they won't stray. Everything else that she watches or reads is littered with dead babies. Stillborn babies, miscarried babies, aborted babies. Have the sex and dead babies always been there, but she never noticed, just as she ignores billboards on road trips? Or is God testing her with malicious intent, manipulating her arousal and then hurling reminders at her of why she must not cave in to temptation? Lucy should be sainted—these mixed cosmic messages are worse than the arrows flung at Sebastian.

Amidst the rampant abstention and Lucy's heroic restraint, Lucy's healthy libido betrays her. A chronic insomniac most of her life, her sleep is deep now, and her dreams vibrant. After several weeks of abstinence, she has a blue dream too explicit even for the X-rated shelf of her mind. She awakens to a powerful orgasm.

The next day, Lucy doesn't know whether she wants to smash or fondle the calculatingly soothing, smooth, round artwork in Dr. Frank's waiting room, the furniture all feminine curves before the rudeness of the exam room. "Everything's fine," Dr. Frank reassures her after she haltingly and euphemistically explains her nocturnal explosion. The tiny heartbeat pulses on the ultrasound. "These preventative measures may be entirely unnecessary. Nothing you do will cause a problem unless you're lifting elephants. We just don't want you to do anything that will cause you to blame yourself if something happens. Better safe than sorry."

Lucy notices the doctor says "miscarriage" about as often as he mentions sex.

♥

A week later, Lucy bleeds, a red river of loss.

Lucy will never crave sex again. Despite the doctor's assurance that nothing Lucy did could have caused the miscarriage, Lucy fears the baby stopped growing out of shock over Mom's bawdy telepathic signals. Deep down she knows that her turgid urges and sailor's vocabulary are not just cause for her sterility. Her baser instincts don't mean she lacks the maternal instinct. Despite her feelings of guilt, she believes she would have been a good mother. And Ian a good father. That they desire each other so profoundly after years together means the promise of a whole, lasting family for their child. A baby girl, Dr. Frank tells her. Lucy names her Grace.

Weeks pass. She cannot remember the last time she felt remotely aroused. Sex will only remind her of what their union cannot bring, of what she wants but cannot have, of what she almost had but lost. She is undesirable. Damaged goods. How can Ian ever be aroused again by the crack in her body when he saw what fell out of it? No longer an erogenous zone, but a war zone. She's gained weight since the miscarriage, her metabolism as slow as a dirge. She feels flabby from her inactivity. Her dull and gray-flecked roots have grown out since her last hair color. Dye isn't recommended for pregnant women, and she can't summon the energy to call her stylist for an appointment now that she can douse her head in chemical baths to her heart's content. Low iron levels exhaust her. Pregnancy hormone mottles her face. Her breasts, back to their normal size, feel tiny and insignificant. When they are touched, she feels irritation, not arousal. If she could only have experienced one orgasm with Ian while they were beckoning, busty, lusty, fully-charged creatures with a hotline wired straight to her groin. Her nipples with their own minds had prank-called the clitoris commissioner all those ceaseless weeks, but now the line is dead. The forfeit of that pleasurable experience is one loss amidst so much loss. She could have had a fuck-fest all that time and it wouldn't have made one fucking bit of difference.

How ironic that desire for sex consumed her during the weeks she could not indulge in pleasures of the flesh, but now—when she could make love 24/7—it's the last thing she wants. Now that her womb is open again for business, lust eludes her.

She has no excuse to refuse Ian. The doctor okays baths, swimming, intercourse, tampons, and exercise. (Linguistically true to form, the nurse wedges sex between mundane activities.) Lucy feels the presence of Ian's cock behind closed doors. He lurks around her with pained desire in his eyes, afraid to pressure her yet needing their union to heal himself—he has lost Grace, too. She misinterprets his respect for her needs as lack of desire for her, confirming her belief that she is no longer appealing—as a fat, ugly, small-breasted woman who apparently will never bear his children. Dr. Frank recommends "mechanical birth control" for a few months—but *she* is mechanical, a robot with no human nerves, and condoms remain a non-issue. Ian remains on the couch. Lucy has no idea how to repair the growing gulf between them.

One night there is a tiny scratching at the bedroom door, with snuffling and high-pitched whining. Startled from the daze she sinks into nightly instead of sleep, she calls out.

"There's someone here to see you." The door muffles Ian's voice.

"I'm not dressed!" Lucy curls up in a corner of the bed, her body shrouded in long flannels.

"He doesn't care." Ian cracks open the door. "Arf arf." Ian is naked. With the hallway light spilling in through the doorway, Lucy makes out his cock—decorated like a Chihuahua. He stands uncertainly, hesitant of Lucy's reaction. She admires him for exposing himself so fully, wholly vulnerable though chances of rejection are high. She snaps on the bedside lamp. Ian has attached two huge ears tied on a soft cord around the shaft and drawn a happy face on the head with a marsh pen, with a red satin bow at the base for a collar and paws drawn on his balls. "I remembered you wanted a ChiWowWow."

Lucy laughs, as much at Ian's inability to pronounce foreign words as at his humor. His mispronunciation was the only thing that ended their argument when they last fought over Lucy's desire for the rat-sized dog, because neither of them could keep a straight face over his ridiculous slaughter of the dog's breed. The murmuring, surprised bubble of her laughter grows inside her until she cackles breathlessly, doubled up on the bed. She laughed like that the night they met, and her unrestrained glee sealed them for life more than the sex that swiftly followed. They could foresee a day far in the future when they would be too old to screw, but never too old to laugh.

Lucy catches her breath. "Man, I needed that. That was better than an orgasm." She hasn't so much as smiled in weeks. Though Ian had tried to make jokes about horny monks and nuns, she hadn't appreciated the humor.

As Ian's cock grows under the glow of Lucy's pleasure, the puppy's face distorts. Ian looks down. "Uh oh. He's drooling."

"Better than piddling. Does he know any commands?"

"Come."

Lucy makes kissy noises and pats the bed. "Come, Loco!"

Ian snuggles next to her on the bed, though her thick nightgown and the blankets separate them. "He likes to be petted."

"I wouldn't want to spoil him."

"There's no such thing as too much love for a puppy."

"His fur is so soft! Oh, dear. He's outgrowing his collar."

"I know a way to fix that." Ian's hand creeps under the blanket, up her gown, and down her panties. He rests the heel of his palm against her mons, his fingers cupped over her mound. At first Lucy winces. Her gash is now a raw wound, not a path to pleasure, but Ian does not nudge her open with his fingers. His hand simply rests low on her belly with only the pressure of its weight. She feels the cold arc of his wedding ring as his palm presses down against her, pushing her own small mound of flesh against her clitoris.

Lucy doesn't know where the orgasm comes from. It mounts inside her and explodes without warning, like a team of Clydesdales tearing around a bend in the road to knock her over. Their thundering, unforeseen passage leaves her sprawled and sloppy on the wayside of unleashed repression, her dress to her face and her hair in damp tangles. The breeze of their stampede dies down, and it is just Lucy and Ian together in the quiet bed.

Lucy blinks at him. "Okay, so maybe laughing isn't better than coming."

Ian smiles. "You can have both. Doctor's orders."

She catches her breath. "I think I needed that."

She cries when Ian crackles the condom packet, symbolizing the prevention of a pregnancy that she so badly wants but that can't be. "You'll suffocate Loco."

"He's a special mutant super-ninja ChiWowWow. He doesn't need air." They kick aside covers and clothing and Ian climbs on top of her. Ian has a hard time gaining entry, partly because he is being so careful, and partly because Lucy is closed like a fist. The condom chafes. "It won't work," Lucy weeps.

"Hold on." Ian squirts half a tube of K-Y between her legs. Her story starts and begins with lubricant. She should purchase stock in the goopy stuff. Lucy laughs.

Ian brushes her cheek. "I love your laugh. I've missed it."

Smeared with jelly, they slide in a slick puddle on the sheets. Ian is cautious and tender. His hesitant entrance hurts at first. "I thought he was a Chihuahua, not a St. Bernard," Lucy gasps. Her vagina creaks, like a swollen door pushed open from its tight frame.

"You okay?" Ian asks. Lucy has forgotten how big and powerful he looks from this perspective, his protective body fully covering hers, when in daily life he is a small man.

"I'm like a virgin." Ian gets his tight fit, after all.

"Remember Sister Cyndy?"

Sister Cyndy, the self-proclaimed Born-Again Virgin who used to preach on the campus lawn where she and Ian first met during his ROTC days. Everything seemed possible, then, except Born-Again Virginity. But it turns out that Sister Cyndy was right. The return of the virginal state *is* possible, yet so much else that seemed possible is not. Lucy remembers the innocence of those days, sitting in the hot sun on the green lawn eating gloppy cafeteria food, when they hadn't yet thought about starting a family, when sex was simple, nothing but the joining of their two young, healthy, and perfect bodies. Sex is loaded now, fraught with repercussions and reminders.

Lucy welcomes the familiar fullness of Ian's body inside hers. There can be nothing sinful about her love of this act. She believes she is a decent person, despite indecent thoughts. She believes in her own goodness despite the lewd locomotive of her mind that pushed her into erotic torment for weeks on end, that broke up the smooth passage of their relationship like train cars derailing, that twisted her like the resulting wreckage into a ball-busting bitch. She believes in her marriage, in the man who won't let her go despite the babies that leaked away.

Another rolling thunderclap unleashes inside her. Her pelvic bone tilted up to Ian's belly as he barely moves, like slow dancing, the orgasm sneaks up on her and bursts.

"Making up for lost time?" Ian brushes the hair from her forehead.

"Shit, that *is* a Wow Wow," Lucy arches and sighs.

"Performs just for you." Sorrow hovers behind their smiles, but they let the hurt pass without sobering the light mood. Ian seems in no hurry for his own pleasure. His cock fills her but doesn't move inside her other than the pulse of his blood. "I love your hair like this. Don't dye it anymore, okay?"

"But all the gray! I'm getting old."

"No, *we're* getting old. Together."

She had lost the baby, orgasms, laughter, and her own personality, but what she missed most was intimacy with Ian. They had always connected and healed through sex. Tonight won't make up for the loss of Grace, she knows, but in this at least she is blessed.

31

Fairy Tail

*W*hy not? If Mutt changed her body, why couldn't I? All the other sea folk spoke the Little Mermaid's name in hushed bubbles, *tsk tsking*. But I call her Mutt. Shorthand for mute, mutated, and mixed breed. The perennial star of our passé piscine show, century to century, culture to culture. Fairy tales, animated kiddy musicals, operas, Daryl Hannah movies, famous statues, yadda yadda. A merlad like me could get sick of having her tail-to-twat saga rubbed in my face—a tale told by the elders to warn me against yearning to be somebody else, somewhere else, but I envied her transformation from scales to skin. They talked like she was the only water-breather besides Neptune who did anything of note. Like she was the only one clever enough to hitch a ride out of the murky, ocean depths. Well, I didn't have Mutt's flawless soprano to trade in for human legs, but I did have something she didn't.

Me, I wasn't sorry Mutt left the ocean for terra firma. I got her sea cave. The mer-tribe avoided her tainted sanctuary, fearing the misfit's curse. But I was spawned discontented, so I wasn't worried. I played with Mutt's barrettes and bikini tops for hours. Mutt bitched about aquatic life for good reason. The makeup sucks. Squid ink can't hold a candle to Revlon, and salt's murder on the complexion.

Mostly, though, Mutt's escape showed me possibilities. You thought she had it bad, wanting feet instead of flippers, but I was born the wrong species *and* the wrong sex. Not only half piscine, half mammalian, but boy body, girl desires. A damn guppy with a mustache instead of mammary glands. Half vertebrate class Osteichthyes and wholly male. Could've been worse, I know. Could've been of the superclass Agnatha, the jawless fishes. They're not called hagfish for nothing.

At least guys on land could express themselves. Cologne, natty slacks, a flamboyant cravat. Less than satisfying if Joe Schmo really wanted ovaries, but at least fashion possibilities existed. Me, I was perennially naked, half epidermis, half scales. Sure, I had a more colorful tail than the girls, but the merchicks could paint their fingernails, stuff their closets with bikini tops and corsets, select coral baubles from overflowing jewelry boxes, garland their hair, pierce their ears. Me? Nada. Zilch. Same weary ho hum day after day unless I wanted to pump up my biceps or sport a fucking Flipper tattoo. All I had was my ass-length hair, which the merfolk elders insisted I cut. The Flotsam Child days ended with the war, they said, and it was time I jettisoned the Age of Aquarius getup.

That was the last straw. The sea king lectured me constantly, not only for my excessive surface time and lack of attention to his daughters (Lord, but we're short on grooms down here—we're teeming with maids but, think about it, how often do you hear about us mer*lads*?), but for my *ways*. Someone tattled about my drag. (I knew who it was, the walleyed son-of-a-bitch, and I got him back when I lured a trawler in his direction. I am nothing if not a master baiter.) Until I cut my hair and buried the lipstick, the king forbade me both the surface and Mutt's cave—I was persona non grotto. Algae covered and miserable, I wanted to throw myself to the sharks.

Between you and me, the king wasn't averse to an occasional feel of boy scales. The giggling nymphs got on his nerves, and he craved an occasional rough and tumble in the sand. Oh, I rolled in the surf with him on occasion, our tails intertwined, but it never amounted to more than a lot of frustrated flapping. He got me pretty sticky, but the salt water washed his enthusiasm right off.

And once I was *dressed*, with my best pearls and my seashell top (and you thought underwire bras were the pits), enticing ships off course. Sunning on a reef with only my torso showing, I was passing, all right. As a girl *and* human. You should have seen the gestures from those sailors! I learned some choice slang.

And then up popped the king, in more ways than one. My excited tail was causing quite an underwater stir. He tackled me without so much as an introduction, and he didn't read me. Hello, can *you* tell the difference between a boy tail and a girl tail? He didn't recognize me with my makeup, either. Thought I was an exotic maid from the other side of the equator. Folks believe what they want to. We frolicked and splashed for hours in the moonlight. He kept trying to cop a feel, but I was too quick for him. My coy silence attracted him (the voice could give a lad away)—a refreshing change for him, since the undersea chatter can be deafening. You try sleeping through the Humpback mating season, and the dolphins aren't much better. Yack yack yack. And just wait until a ship passes the Sirens. Their racket could rupture an eardrum! Later on, I would catch the king looking wistful up on that reef.

I had my own human prince, too. Mutt's not the only one with a regal lover. Shipwrecked nobility's a dime a dozen. How many princes getting washed overboard does it take for humans to get it? You'd think they'd learn to lash those pretty boys to the deck. Keep 'em safe, plus they'd get into light bondage—kinky, inbred aristocracy's no secret. And did you ever notice our fairy tale's the only one where the *guy* gets rescued? No wonder my gender orientation's all screwed up.

So, anyway, there was my drowning beefcake, clinging to a rock. I didn't know at the time if he was heir to any throne, but he had a most princely package. He was newt, I mean nude, stripped naked by the turbulent waters of desire (i.e., me) and in need of resuscitation. Could I help it if I latched onto the first appendage available? He came to life, in more ways than one. The piscine pecker remains private no matter the stage of ecstasy, but this transformation...a jellyfish turned into a dolphin snout! Holy mackerel! My tail *ached*. Not to have such a sea snake, but to have one *inside me*.

The prince woke up. It was love at first sight on his part. All he could see was the top of my bobbing head and my long hair floating with the current, so let's say my personality won him over. I kept him on that rock a couple of days, having sport with him. But, like all fairy tale creatures, he pined for his own kind, and I had to carry him home.

He knew what I was, in one respect. When he arched his back and latched his legs around me, his little submarine could only slide against my scales. And there's the irony. Humans idolize mermaids as sexual beings, the pinnacle of erotic imagery. But it's all slippery foreplay. Hello, dudes, there's nowhere to *put your love thang.* It's, like, so obvious. Mer*maid.* Get it? Read eternal virgin. Duh. *What* are you mortal boys all *thinking?*

But my prince didn't know that even without the tail, my body lacked a lady's accommodating seam. That my bikini top covered only handfuls of seaweed. That he kissed boy lips, artfully painted and which he dutifully smudged with sloppy passion. That my slim hips were due to more than late pubescence. That what he thought was my clitoris was actually a shining example of the well-camouflaged piscine penis. Think about it: have you even *seen* one on a whale? No matter the size, the sleek design is most accommodating to *my* designs. For which I'm grateful. I never had to go to the uncomfortable lengths of disguise as my protruding human counterparts, poor dears. Try hiding a torpedo in your lace panties. O*w.*

I never confessed the truth to my princely lover. The human male might lust after a little inter-species or even extra-terrestrial intercourse, especially when their sexually-aggressive she-lover's on top, but threaten their fragile heterosexual masculinity and, girlfriend, you're in trouble. You catch my drift.

Maybe you're thinking that I wasn't a boy trapped in a girl's body. Maybe I was just *that way*. You know, limp-wristed. My scales rippled when I watched pirates and their cabin boys, sure. I'd take it over a tail. But I wanted the Carmen dress. The red lipstick, gypsy earrings, and fishnet stockings. If my legs were going to ache with the dagger slice of their magic creation, then my feet might as well kill me in heels.

With talk of a buzz cut and marriage to Mutt's sister looming, I was ruining my nails with worry. I had to act quickly. There's no deep sea, sex reassignment surgery, honey. Just wands and spells. And I intended to use them. If that damn Mutt with her incessant humming could splice her way to happiness like an Oscar-winning film editor, then why couldn't I? If the old sea witch, Jezibaba, could put a hole between Mutt's new legs, why not mine? While I went about morphing into a mammal down there, why should I have to sprout a sea cucumber instead of excavating a cave?

It's not like Mutt has all the necessary equipment. They talk about Happily Ever After, but all she can do is squirt out caviar. She got the bearded clam, but not the indoor plumbing, and Mutt's prince needed an heir. Nobody's gotten the ending right—not Hans Christian, not Walt, not Dvorak. I felt sorry for her. She crept out at night to bury her eggs in the sand. Kissed by moonlight and sea foam, they turned into phosphorescent pearls. Mutt's put on weight, too. You can't blame a girl. Éclairs are a damn sight better than plankton.

But what to give up in my quest for not only knees, but a pussy instead of a penis? Trading scales for snatch requires more than a Gold card. I can't carry a tune to save my life, so trading my voice for a vulva like Mutt wasn't an option. Nor would I trade my hair, long and luxurious, my key to passing as a damsel. If a mullet-cut was to be my fate, I'd rather keep my gills and marry the eldest daughter. Not my pretty features, my green eyes, nuh uh. I wasn't of the nobility—I was a poor serf—so what could I offer in exchange for the proverbial knife? I conceived of an idea.

The sea witch was happy to see me. Since she was responsible for Mutt's now being a mute, overweight, and infertile Homo sapien, the king forbade any intercourse with her, talking or touching. And there was the problem. There were no undersea sperm donor banks, and Jezibaba's biological clock was ticking. She could morph life, but she couldn't create it except for the old fashioned way. She required a Daddy to help her hatch some eggs. She needed some fertilizer and she needed some *bad*. Her eyes lit up at my proposition, and she took my bait. We shook fins on our deal.

So I blew my wad before I lost the spout. Milked myself right into an oyster shell. The prospect of my new body so excited me that I donated a healthy supply. Beats spilling my guts ad nauseam to a therapist to get the sex change stamp of approval.

Jezibaba was touched by my gift of a turkey baster. I mean, *ew*, you didn't think I was going to flop around with her in the shallows, did you? She was already in the family way as I floated away to my new terrestrial destiny.

The waves tossed me on shore as a stark naked human female. Jezibaba in her gratitude outdid herself. "Make 'em big, Jezzy," I had told her. "If I'm gonna do this, I don't want no *A* cup." I've got wide shoulders, and my knockers needed to look proportionate.

Now, I'm no dummy. I didn't wash up on a deserted beach in a fairy tale, where there's only one good catch, like it's the prince or the stable boy. *Please.* That is so twentieth century. No bottom fishing for me. This girl's entrance would be a splash. Praise be waterproof mascara.

I chose Miami Beach in broad daylight. Who should be tanning himself as I rose out of the foam but the modeling agent for Cindy *Craw*ford (you tell me she doesn't have a secret past with a name like that). I knew he was vacationing there—I watched *Entertainment Tonight* on passing cruise ships. He landed me a contract and popped my cherry, too—*after* we signed on the dotted line. More fun than a cold and clinical vaginal dilator for keeping a new well drilled.

Now I walk the catwalks of Paris and New York. I'm so famous that people know me by one name, Merléné. Mutt got a scum-slick statue in Copenhagen, but I got the cover of *Vogue*. You wouldn't believe my net income. My fan club members are quite the fawning groupers. Critics predict that my career will flounder, but, *tthhpptt*, I don't age! My managers keep me out of the sun, to preserve that "effervescent sheen" the photographers rave over, though they complain that I squirm. I've been called captivating, enchanting, and

39

mysterious, with other-worldly good looks. I know how to angle for a compliment. If they only knew what used to pulse beneath my thong. They long for my autobiography, but that's a tail no one will believe.

It's not that I don't miss the sea sometimes. More than one lover has told me I undulate excessively in the sack. I'm hyper-sensitive about references to a fishy odor, though I'm told this is normal. Once when I was drunk I let out that I was piscine. What a gaff! But my date thought I said Episcopalian. Another guy thought I meant my astrological sign. Like I said, folks believe what they want.

Sometimes I ache for my tail. Mine was gorgeous. The male of the species always lucks out that way. My iridescent green scales glowed in peacock colors when I was aroused, which was constantly, especially in front of mirrors. The sea king surely knew whom he tried to harpoon that magic night under the stars. He grounded me because he knew I would transform myself and leave. Perhaps I would have stayed if he had embraced me as I was. But he couldn't confess that he had gaping gills over another guy, especially one dressed in a soggy bustier. He has his kingdom to consider, after all, and his fins can only flutter publicly for females. Too bad. He could use a queen. But that was his aquatic quandary, and I've gone on with my life. I can never go back.

I skinny-dipped under the moonlight recently. I nearly drowned, not knowing how to swim without my tail, but the king's virile hands buoyed and groped me. Finally, those manly monarch fingers full of my real breasts. No padded bikini-top this time. No coy darting away like a shy school girl. And if there's one thing a merman knows how to play with, it's nipples, 'cause there's not much else to titillate. We mated properly, as male and female, and his trident was impressive enough as far as fish privates go. Size matters, honey, and to say otherwise is a phallus-y. But I didn't make comparisons when he swam with me wrapped in his embrace, tasting the glory of cresting moments, surfing the tides of love. My ass crack leaked sand for an eternity afterwards, though, and from now on it's a mattress or abstention.

She tricked me, the old sea cow did, and left me with my facial hair. But I watched the Shopping Channel and knew what to order to permanently eliminate the five o'clock shadow. There's always a catch to these spells, but I have technology on my side.

I got Jezzy back. I snatched one of her brood. She laid 28 million, so it's not like she couldn't spare one. I sent little Moses in his basket down Mutt's river. Mutt worked some deal to transform her adoptive son's tentacles into human limbs. Hey, I've got my Mother Teresa moments, but I left a red herring so she wouldn't know I was the do-gooder. I don't want to mix up her *G* rating with my *R* story. Besides, I'd have to coo over the little tyke. I got the fashion instinct, not the maternal instinct. Frankly, I'm glad I didn't get the indoor plumbing. No PMS! Other than the lingering effects of Piscine Mammalian Syndrome, of course.

As for my washed-up, human prince? He turned out to be the bona fide castle type, with magnificent jewels in his treasure chest as well as in his knickers. I pay clandestine visits, for which he's grateful. His marriage to a flighty swan has been less than satisfactory. But I'm not about to base my happiness on the whim of one fickle, horny bastard. Those other fairy tale chicks required the true love of one man for their transformations. Screw that old fashioned bullshit. Cast a wide net, I say. Keep one in every port, above and below water. This girl intends to have it all, on her terms. I'd like to say I used my brains, but it all comes back to using a cock, doesn't it? But the phallus is what I gave up. Not what saved me. And I don't intend to base my future on needing one again. This media goddess will gladly spread her legs for homage, but not for salvation. I don't need beast, phantom, jungle boy, knight, or vampire to awaken me. My eyes are wide open, honey, and I'm biting the queen's apple.

London Derrière

*N*ever perform with your back to the audience, Orlando taught his rare music students (he took on such commitments only when financially strapped). Shake your booty if you've got Jon Bon Jovi's can, he instructed, its leather-enshrined splendor made manifest across vast arenas. But if you're a mere mortal crooning in a local pub, best to face the fans.

How, then, did Orlando come to find himself bent over a barstool on the stage floor—nothing more than a bar corner cleared of tables—with Isabella humping his middle-aged, virgin ass? His back to the audience, indeed.

Orlando now sang a different tune than the melodic ones he'd played for the small audience of late-nighters. His voice lost its smooth patina. His words contained no witty double entendres, looping rhymes, or seductive repetitions. He abandoned his lyrical search for meaning in a complicated world of misunderstood words. His fingers no longer picked at intricate chord progressions on the six-string or electric keyboard. They clawed at the air. He growled and shouted, his words incomprehensible, pushing back against Isabella's thrusting thighs. But before he descended into passionate, guttural urges, his words were clear.

Orlando feared the peculiar combination of words he shouted. He was terrified that, once uttered, Isabella would have what she wanted and leave him. Again. Only this time she would desert him for speaking the irretrievable, and not for silence.

Hold something back, Orlando taught. Leave the fans wanting, so they return, or, better yet, purchase the compact disc you've peddled for years, stacks of them stashed in your attic. The whole song can't be a repeating chorus, he instructed. You've got to build up to the consummate word at the end of the line. A literary crescendo to a word so perfect that the audience thinks they could have guessed it, but a word so unexpected they never do. They echo it once they've heard the song, and then forget the wonder and surprise of it. Like this word he just enunciated as clearly as the *Rain in Spain* before deteriorating into whimpering gibberish. A word that all-too-often atrophied, stalled, and lost its meaning through overuse. A powerful word that dulled and tired. Coveting words, understanding their potency and deception, he had refused to utter it all these years.

Now that he'd said it, held nothing back, Isabella would leave him with his woody testing the barroom air like a blind man brandishing his cane at a cliff's edge. One clench of his fist and Orlando would add to the stains on the floor. Isabella hadn't told him not to touch himself, though she often commanded him in bed.

Orlando himself was never comfortable articulating what he wanted done to his body, and he graciously accepted what was offered. But right now he wanted his satisfaction—if she planned to give him any—to come at her hands, the gift of her body. He'd had enough of his own joyless onanism since she kicked him out a month ago.

As Isabella brought up the rhythm section behind him, the logistical success of this joint venture amazed Orlando. But, then again, they'd always enjoyed the challenge of different body sizes. He tended to forget how small she was. Her posterior gave her such solidity, a gravity-hugging mass—like a steel girder that holds up a delicate bridge, one of those impossible pieces of architecture that tourists traverse the world to see—that he often forgot that his long fingers could nearly span her waist, a delicate apex flaring out to a remarkable triangle. His shirts hung past her knees. Sometimes when he spied her tiny shoes kicked off at the front door, he wondered who'd come to visit.

Isabella's ass. Now there was a show fit for stadium concerts. Forget the rules about facing the audience. Her magnificent flesh danced in multiple directions when she moved, her crack a Continental Divide. Some law of physics or aerodynamics caused one hemisphere of her buttocks to return from movement while its opposing sector gained momentum in the opposite direction, the way two stones tossed in a pond throw concentric circles into delirium. Her gluts were like tectonic plates beneath the earth's surface, the mountains above them trembling and quaking when they shifted.

When Orlando was still a young man, years before Isabella backed her ancient Cadillac into his Toyota, one of his dates had blubbered over the televised wedding of the worthless son who stood second-in-line to the worthless British crown. Somewhere in her tears Orlando saw the crushed belief that even though the first-born prince had escaped her, the second son had still roamed in her fantasies as a distinct possibility. She, an American. From Detroit. He had waited impatiently for the "I Do's" so they could head to dinner. Then he'd caught sight of the paired jewels shimmering beneath the oversized satin bow perched on the bride's tailbone. He could have watched the newly-minted princess march up the aisle for miles. He wanted to reach up inside her gown and caress Her Royal Heinie, to crawl after that fanny through the church and into eternity, groping the *royal we*. Her tush wasn't even *that* big, except in comparison to Barbie dolls like her new sister-in-law. When radio deejays later made derisive jokes about her flanks, Orlando knew that not one of those mocking men would turn down the chance to have the princess climb aboard his dime store wand. Orlando suspected their taunting was born of insecurity—a peon peter could seem awfully small and insignificant rutting beneath such a queenly throne. Orlando thanked whatever cosmic force had blessed him with the long and narrow scepter ideal for such knightly devotion. He would gladly plant his flag for the sovereign, claiming mountainous territory. The sun would never set on his all-conquering passion.

Orlando and his date never did get to dinner that night. They ordered in, and he had barbecued rump roast right in her bed. It wasn't the start of a fetish, exactly, or even an obsession. Orlando liked women of all sizes—but big-hipped women became synonymous with royalty in his plebian mind. That bow on a princess's palatial behind tied a permanent knot around his preference, and he remained married to the idea of someday finding his own monarchial mounds to revere.

But Orlando soon learned that these splendid endomorphs didn't crave worship of the twin-buttressed cathedrals on their backsides. Rather, they wished to eradicate these sacred temples, as ancient peoples had demolished shrines glorifying opposing religions. They wanted to destroy these icons of femininity, smash the twin tablets on their backs, praying for the holiness of honed and toned hind-ends. They strove to conjure a mythological Atlantis in their mirrors. They believed sleek columns shimmered beneath their ripples, if only they sacrificed enough to their belief in lean and inhospitable flanks. They wanted Orlando not to pay homage to the bouncing embodiments of his faith, as he wished, but to ignore them, averting his eyes as one does from airport Hare Krishnas.

When the princess crash dieted later on and became the spokesperson for a diet product, Orlando composed a dirge. Her lost flesh symbolized the war waged upon the tortured landscape of women's curves, a genocidal campaign for the extermination of something holy. His lovers all felt rotten about not being Twiggy. He craved the sight of their haunches wriggling, but these ripe, succulent women extinguished the lights and crawled under the covers, face up in the dark. Which is why, with the passage of years, he seldom followed through on his attraction for them. He swore them off, a gluteus abstinence, the way friends with wheat allergies had given up gluten. Their constant need for reassurance wore him down. They vacuumed up his repeated compliments, and then ceased to believe them precisely because of their repetition. Ah, the trickiness of words.

Then Isabella had climbed out of her mammoth automobile a few years ago after reversing into his hatchback. When she leaned back into her car to dig her insurance card out of the glove box, her derrière sticking out of the car door, Orlando swooned. Such an ass could sing opera. No Butterfly pining for her straying dude, but a fierce Turandot demanding the severed heads of unworthy suitors. Orlando stuttered so ferociously when she approached that Isabella thought he'd had a concussion from the minor accident. He'd bruised his forehead on the steering wheel with her lurch into reverse, yes—but all he wanted was to smash his face against those cheeks, just the way his hood had crumpled under the staggering weight of the Cadillac's trunk. He wanted bumper imprints ground into his deliriously smiling front grille. He reminded himself that he had given up on these women, swore them off in a permanent Lent. He no longer prayed to their vaulted chambers. The simplicity of a glorious derrière had too often trapped him in complicated and ugly arguments. When he wanted a fistful of those mounds, he usually got an earful about his inability to understand. He didn't blame them for their insecurity; they were the victims of a modern witch hunt for body fat. But despite his devotion to their ample order, Orlando could not resurrect a religion based on his cock alone, and so went on a flesh fast.

He could have abstained 'til death do him part, he lied to himself, if Isabella hadn't spoken in that damned accent, refined aristocratic education crossed with Monty Python crass in her Oxford-gutter mouth. A dethroned British queen had backed into him, and he wanted her to keep backing up, rolling her awesome bulldozer of a behind right into his lap. His inseam bulged so prominently that he refused to get out of his squashed bug of a car, worried his woody'd get caught in the rack and pinion. She feared that he couldn't extricate himself from the interlocking, twisted metal of the two cars, and it was true in a way—her rear end had trapped his heart. His lustful frame of mind was permanently bent to her shape.

The dreadful sound of the two vehicles wrenching apart, Isabella with her foot on the gas, this time in first gear, was not as painful as the silence after she drove him out the front door last month, suitcase and guitar in hand.

She drove him home that first afternoon, but said she was so rattled she needed to stop for a drink. She declared he looked like he needed one, too. She drank her double whiskey in regular cola, "None of that diet crap," she warned the bartender.

After three beers and a shot himself, Orlando couldn't help it: he began to hum *Londonderry Air*. Making the words up on the spot, the revised *London Derrière* began spilling out. She might have socked him in the jaw, but instead she laughed, delighted. She dragged him onto the dance floor and gyrated, her back against him. This time he could not hide his eager gear shift behind a collapsed dash. They hooked together like a tow-hitch and its load. He wrote her a new song on each anniversary of their crash. *Do the Locomotive With Me. Fanny Fandango. Mother Goose Your Caboose. Keister Kabob. Let's Cause a Rumpus.* The songs were for her only, hymns performed during private services to her body. But on their fifth anniversary, she didn't want a song. She wanted a three-word sentence. When he couldn't comply, she gave him not her booty, but the boot.

He admired the way she dressed—or didn't. Not attired in a flowery potato-sack to hide her figure or a low-necked blouse to distract from the rest of her. No futile attempts to disguise the fact that she wore a jeans size in double digits, twice her shirt size. "Vertical stripes aren't going to fucking fool anybody," she said, not that she cared to. She wore bold colors, bright patterns, and snug fits. Not tight or restrictive, but contoured to her shape. Mostly, though, Isabella went naked, stripping with relief as soon as she got home.

Isabella didn't need convincing or wooing to bend over for him. After cocktails, she took him to her house without asking where he wanted to go. Bedroom curtains open, Isabella offered herself like one of those monkeys on the Discovery Channel. He approached the twin celestial planets that orbited around her fiery core with reverential hands. Just as he had once caressed Jimi Hendrix's left-handed guitar, the curves so like Isabella's; as he had stroked the Buddha's belly in China; as he had held his first erection in wonder and terror. He broke Lent. He lost his rocket in her cosmic folds, a tiny spaceship careening through her vortex. A puckered crater winked up at him from between her double moons.

With the lights blazing, he watched his fingers digging into her hips, circles of white spreading from his grip. Like denting a tender peach, or watching the impression of his foot haloing out on wet sand. He gripped that jiggling love handle on her roller coaster. He reached around to lolling breasts and thighs spread just right for easy access to the magic spot so many men, apparently, ignored. Why? It was so simple. He'd seen the way women worked over his dick, with mouth, hand, or body. Jesus, making him come took *effort*. But he could just lay back, one arm under his head, and move a single finger. Even a pinkie. Even a goddamn toe positioned just right, though it tended to cramp up on him if she took awhile—and Isabella was never one to hurry. Yeah, sometimes it was an afterthought—face it, he could be as quick and eager as the next guy, he was no god—but the gesture was one they sure appreciated.

Orlando carefully kept one of his fingers uncalloused. His love digit, Isabella christened it. All it takes is one, his first girlfriend had taught him, a piece of knowledge that had served him better than anything he'd learned in college. Keep it clean and well-trimmed, she'd said, and that way you can put it just about anywhere. Later, after he'd picked up the steel-string and welts of protective skin cropped up all over his hands, he left one fingertip smooth. Only good for picking his nose, he told his vapid-eyed music students. It hampered complicated riffs, but the sacrifice was worth it.

Like the perfect lyric, Isabella continued to surprise him. Unlike the girdle-ish contraptions he found other women trapped in, Isabella wore thong underwear—when she wore any at all. She claimed panties wouldn't fit her, other than the suffocating type she

51

had no interest in wearing. Instead of plucking at elastic that rode up uncomfortably into her crevices, she let it all hang out. Her undies were no more than a swatch of fabric that cupped her *mons*, and a string that nestled where Orlando wished his tongue could take up permanent residence.

Isabella let him watch her shower, the soap disappearing between the cleavage of her thighs. She bathed belly-down in the oversized tub she'd remodeled the house around, her mounds looking like twin atolls rising out of the bubbly deep. Amelia Earhart's plane could vanish in that landscape. Isabella declared she would never need a tattoo, since Orlando's ass hickeys permanently decorated her. He couldn't help nibbling his devotion, a taking of the sacrament. As soon as one love bite faded, he replaced it with another. She backed up to mirrors, contorting impossibly as she tried to find Rorschach meaning in their patterns.

On the rare occasions when Orlando refused to be distracted from practicing by her undulating waves of desire, Isabella practiced naked yoga in his line of vision. Her wide-hulled boat continually capsized during the balancing poses. His will power couldn't surmount such a tidal effect, and before she'd toppled over a third time, he gave in to temptation and righted her with his sturdy mast.

He'd been surprised when she'd packed his things a month ago. (There was no question as to who would stay, since he could never ask her to give up the bathtub.) She abdicated the throne he'd constructed beneath her. Left him a country-less peasant, an expatriate wandering through the pages of disappointing swimsuit issues, where big-boobed gazelles pranced through his Humpback fantasies. All because of one word. One stupid word. What a tragic irony, fit for an opera, that his song lyrics had wooed Isabella to him, but his silence in response to her demand had driven her away.

Dumping him looked good on her. He couldn't take his eyes off her once he'd spotted her precariously perched on a barstool tonight. He wanted to metamorphose into that stool. She looked like she'd swallowed the goddess she always sprinkled into casual conversation. She looked powerful. She looked like trouble. Dressed to kill in a red Empire-waist dress that cinched her bodice but flared out at the hips and fell past her knees, she looked like the Great Pyramid. Not one of the Egyptian priestesses mummified inside, no, but a live monument pulsing with desert sunlight, stretching to the sky yet rooted on earth, radiating heat.

Isabella always looked damned hot walking away. Trailing behind her at the mall or the market, admiring her bouncing globes, Orlando often felt he would have been a better student with such visual aids.

But Isabella looked even better coming back towards him.

"Isabella." He spread his hands when she approached him after the last song. She needn't have waited so politely—she was an audience of one.

"You're an asshole," she said in her irresistible accent.

"I know." He would do or say anything tonight to get her back.

"No, you don't. I'm going to make you *feel* the meaning of asshole. So that next time you'll think twice before using it on someone else."

"Hey, I did *not* shit on you."

"No, because you're emotionally constipated." She seemed surprised by her own wit.

He spied the crack in her slammed door, the thin moment where he could sneak in and make her forget her anger. "Can I use that in a song?"

"Always a joke. Always your music." She hung on to her resentment, leveraging herself against the other side of the door, her side of the argument. "Always detachment. Reserve. Calculation. Tonight I'm breaking your barrier. Drop your pants." But she lifted her skirt, exposing herself to the waist.

"Jesus." His mouth dropped open, not his 501s. Amidst curlicues of wiry hair (for she also refused the pain of waxing), Isabella had sprouted a penis. It seemed as if their entire courtship had been a build-up to the lyrical surprise of the pink and white swirled cock *sproinging* from beneath her uplifted dress. Strapped on with a complicated series of belts and buckles, the cock appeared lifelike in shape, if not in color. The straps looked damned uncomfortable, cutting into her generous flesh. He admired her ease with the contraption. Most women of her build wouldn't be caught dead in a bikini, much less this get-up. Her customary thong would have proven entirely inadequate to the task of restraining the hungry beast.

"Isabella, what the hell do you want?"

"I want your hymen."

Hi, men! His mind spun spellings and alternate definitions. His mental word play always got worse when he was nervous, a subconscious tic he couldn't control. "Whoa, whoa, whoa."

54

"I want your cherry. Your maidenhead."

He stepped backwards, away from the threatening member. "This is a joke, right?"

"You're looking at the punch-line." She took the hefty pink cock in her small fist. "Take a good look while you can, because you're not going to be seeing much of it in a minute."

Ironically, Isabella had never seemed more womanly than with this jutting member thrusting forward from her thighs, her queenly power visibly concentrated in this vengeful sword. Orlando was hot. Inflamed. Also terrified. Unlike him, Isabella always said what she meant and meant what she said.

"Isabella. Christ. Here?" He glanced around the deserted bar. The bartender had started to set the chairs on the tables halfway through Orlando's last set. His mediocre and distracted performance once he'd caught sight of Isabella in the audience had encouraged few to remain through to the last number. The bartender had waved goodnight before Orlando's last note faded on his new song, *My Expat Ex*. The bartender called out for Orlando to lock up on his way out, adding that he'd mop in the morning, unless Orlando wanted to do it for extra cash.

"All the better if someone sees you for the butthead that you are," Isabella said.

"Fine! Fine." Orlando tore at his belt buckle and thrashed his pants to his ankles. "I'll play your little game. Whatever you want, Isabella." He turned his back to her before lowering his boxers, so she couldn't see his eager state. Orlando didn't know if he was angrier at Isabella or at the betrayal of his own dick, which rose up in direct opposition to what he thought he didn't want. But he did know that he wanted her to stay, to connect with her. On any level. He bent over the barstool he'd perched on for his show. "Come and get it." He didn't think she'd do it.

Her dress rustled as she stepped close behind him. He smelled her, an oasis of bubble-bath clean in a stale swamp of cigarette smoke and beer.

"You know what I want," she said, the tip of her dick kissing his delicate pucker.

"Why is it so important?" he shouted over his shoulder. "Christ, you *know* how I feel. Isn't it more important that I *show* it? *Express* it? Don't I do that?"

She pressed deeper. "I want you to say it."

He grunted. "It can't possibly mean the same thing to different people."

"You're holding back out of fear. Just like with your music. You won't commit the last three percent. That's why you're still playing dives like this."

"We've been over this a thousand times. It's worthless to say it."

She continued her nudging insistence. "I know it's what you feel. Just say it."

"It's meaningless if you have to ask."

"It's everything."

He made an incoherent noise as she slipped in a centimeter, then another. Isabella still worked with metrics.

"It won't kill you," she said. "Don't be afraid."

"I'm done talking. You...uhn, you just do what you have to do to make your point."

"I'm not stopping 'til you say it."

Crafty Isabella had just thwarted herself. Orlando didn't want her to stop. Considering his preoccupation with rear ends, it now struck him as odd that he'd never given much thought to his own. His morning post-coffee toiletries and a vigorous daily scrubbing were all the attentions he'd ever thought of bestowing upon it.

"You're pressuring me," he quipped, disguising his level of enjoyment with the sort of response that had incited her to this in the first place.

She slapped his thigh. "Giddyap. Say it."

Orlando was silent.

Slowly Isabella worked her slippery manhood in. She was being careful, he could tell, cautious not to really hurt him. His cheeks now pressed firmly beneath the swell of her belly. The front of her thighs nudged the back of his. Her high-heeled feet, calculated for the height she would need for this maneuver, were wedged between his scuffed cowboy boots, swathed with his jeans and boxers like the base of a Christmas tree. The hem of her dress tickled his lower back. Orlando had never experienced the blindness of having someone make love to him from behind, never felt the surprise of every touch by their hands or body. Isabella often mounted him while he lay on his back, telling him to hold still until she'd used him for her own friction, but he could still participate, teasing between her legs or massaging her breasts, communicating with facial expressions. This was powerlessness of another order. Total abandon, at her mercy. An absolute trust and giving of oneself. And she had done it so boldly, so baldly, so often.

She grabbed his scant hips, and leaned over to whisper in his ear. "Say it."

Orlando pushed back against her.

Isabella switched gears. Her breath changed to short pants of hot steam on his back. Her movements became more calculated. She had gone from anger to arousal. He sensed her surprise, that this fucking would afford her pleasure, too. She picked up her pace, forgot the metric system and took a quantum leap. Isabella gave him her last three percent.

She grabbed his hair. "Say it!" She punctuated her repeated demand with the insistent sound of her belly slapping against his cheeks. If someone had peeked through the steamy front windows into the dim bar, all they would have seen was the flapping red tent of her dress, the spread wings of an exotic bird.

Orlando opened his mouth but couldn't catch his breath.

"I love you," Isabella said softly. She broke through his barrier with her thrusts.

"I…Damn, I love you, too." Orlando half sobbed. She burst a dam within him. A massive, concrete structure that had allowed only trickles of truth to get through, leaving those on the other side thirsty and parched. The granite crumbled, and years of pent-up, churning water deluged the desert. "I do. I really do."

Isabella abruptly stilled.

"Don't stop! Don't."

"Say it. Say it."

"Jesus," he bit his lip. "I fucking love you. I fucking love you. Let me love you."

She was right about his music, about everything. He had cassette tapes crammed with serious songs. Lyrics that expressed his ache and longing and, yes, his love. But he feared they were sappy, that he would be laughed at, and so he made laughter at his humorous songs a certainty. No risk. Isabella's thrusts knocked those tunes loose, setting free a flock of singing birds in his head. Stored up inside him for years now, they tumbled out.

"I love you, I love you, I love," he said, in time with her thrusts. She arced. He knew her sounds, could tell how close she was. She slapped against him, harder and faster. He was full of her. And he couldn't believe it, but he was coming, too. Without a touch from her on his front doorknob, he cried, and came, shouting that he loved her. They stood shuddering. The red dress shimmered with the trembling of their joined bodies.

She nibbled on his shoulder, her arms tight around his belly, her breasts smashed against his back. He didn't want this moment to end. He wanted their bodies to remain entwined. He wanted her to take up residence inside him. Except that then he would never have another good look at her glorious derrière.

Jennifer D. Munro

The Dogs of Sayulita

Dogs. Everywhere. Filthy, mangy, skinny mongrels. They pant in the scarce shade. They scratch at fleas in the pitted, dirt road. The taxi driver almost hits a few roaming mutts as they amble out of the way in the dusty heat. Used to operating on life's margins, like the villagers themselves, the dogs know exactly how slowly they can meander yet still avoid impact with hurtling bumpers. Lacking street smarts, several three-legged dogs miscalculated. Evolution would eliminate the faulty canine gene pools. But what, Emma wonders, did Darwin have against her and Devon's lineage? Will their marriage, a family tree with shallow roots, topple in the drought of childlessness?

The taxi driver speeds north from the Puerta Vallarta airport to the bayside hamlet of Sayulita. He passes on blind curves along the narrow, jungle road. His bumper tosses a pedestrian's skirt. Emma sits mute in the back seat, hair flying like Medusa's snakes from the wind that whips through the open windows. She can't buckle the

60

broken seatbelt. Devon haggled this deal of a ride instead of paying full fare for an air-conditioned four door. She wishes he'd splurged for her sake, but understands his frugality. They can ill-afford this unplanned vacation, more a convalescence than a holiday. Though Amanda had lent them her vacation home in a town they couldn't locate on the tourist map, the last minute airfare had been astronomical, and they had wiped out their savings on the unsuccessful in-vitro treatments. They could hardly afford dinner at the local Taco Bell, much less a trip to Mexico.

The taxi driver almost clips a petrol tanker. Emma envisions, almost desires, a spectacular Hollywood movie blast. She wouldn't mind meeting her end in dramatic flame. At least it would be something. She's as numb as her anesthetized womb when the doctor inserted the fertilized eggs—all claustrophobic guppies who high-tailed it downriver rather than bask on her welcoming shore.

Devon sits in the passenger seat babbling in bad Spanish with the driver, dredging up words from freshman year. Devon contemplates adventure, not mortality, a trait that both attracts and annoys Emma. She had worried about how he would adapt to fatherhood. He gesticulates wildly, as if he can grab forgotten words out of the air. He calls the small town they travel to "Salsalito," no doubt confirming the ignorance of all *gringos* in the driver's mind. But the driver encourages Devon's attempt to converse in the native language. Emma wishes her husband would shut up and let the man concentrate on the winding road rather than puzzling over Devon's garbled queries. Thrilled, Devon translates the driver's assertion that wild tigers haunt the jungle. Emma suspects he means housecats.

A stoplight provides momentary relief from the rush towards mangled death. A horde of dirty children swarms the car, begging. One kid is missing an arm. The driver barks something in rushed syllables that pile swiftly one on top of the other, and peels out.

They approach a military checkpoint, where guards with sweaty hands clutch bazookas. Belts of ammunition crosshatch their stiff bodies. Emma tries to look nonchalant, with her best *nothing in the trunk, sir,* expression, then wonders if overtly acting *not guilty* causes suspicion. The driver mutters, but they cruise through without being stopped.

They drive up and down the cratered streets of Sayulita searching for Amanda's house. "Now, it's not a luxury resort or anything," Amanda had warned. They hadn't believed her. They'd seen what kind of wine she stocked at her lakefront home. She wasn't the type for rustic vacation shacks. But they bounce and jolt through the rundown town, chased by clouds of dust. Rather than snap at the taxi driver to take her back to the airport, Emma focuses on the dogs of Sayulita. They look content despite a miserable existence. They doze in lazy harmony, too hot and hungry to worry about defending meager territories. Odd Chihuahua mixes curl up beside strange Great Dane-like creatures. No breed segregation here. Rampant fornication had produced abundant, bizarre results. Emma pictures a miniature mutt perching his spindly hind legs on a splintered packing crate to reach his towering mate. Or, the other way around, how would a Lab penis fit in a poodle puss? Wouldn't it get stuck? How could they find the energy to screw in this heat, anyway?

What strikes Emma, though, is not so much the canine quantity and variety, but the balls. Countless swollen nuts sway between bony legs. Starving pooches haul ripe appendages, like stoic tramps dragging their bulging rucksacks. Emma is surrounded by an army of unsnipped doggie testicles. The obscene display of unchecked gonads transfixes her.

Only stray children outnumber the dogs. They wander the street or huddle under makeshift awnings, without adult supervision. Two boys in a crispy, brown field practice with lassos. The older child snares his patient dog, which doesn't budge as the rope tightens around its drooping neck. A naked baby crawls through the dirt. Emma the Mama Bandita could snatch the infant, *una desperada* propelled by an estrogen rush. But she doesn't have the will to open the car door, much less make a run for the border. She doesn't know what she wants, anymore.

Amanda's house is, of course, lovely, once they find it, an oasis of luxury in the third-world town. A pure water dispenser protects them from bacterial harm. The three-room *casa* is a perfect setup for the perfect family vacationing in the tropics, with a king-sized bed for the doting parents, a double bed for the sullen teenager, and twin beds for the two youngest. Emma shuts the doors on the two smaller rooms.

Ceiling fans beat a lazy tempo throughout the house. Two walls of the main living *sala* consist entirely of accordion doors that fold back like a giant fan, opening the house to the breeze. Emma tugs, but the salty heat has swollen the dark wood. Devon wrestles them open, and they step to the outside *palapa*. A thatched roof shades the patio. A bumblebee on steroids, ignorant of its carefree pollinating, flits from pink to red bougainvillea flowers that drape the walls. Heavy fruit loads the coconut trees lining the walkway. The warm waters of the Pacific Ocean slap at the beach, mere steps away. With the doors open, their living room is practically an extension of the beach.

Later, dozing on the couch, Emma opens her eyes and sees a spout of mist in the distance. A second, smaller puff mimics the first. A mama whale, traveling back north with her newborn calf. Emma sits up. "Damn it, I need a drink. I don't care what kind of contaminated water's in the ice." Emma hasn't had a glass of wine in months, booze eliminated from her diet as one more possible conception-inhibitor. "I sterilize my laboratory with alcohol. It kills everything," the lab technician who mated Devon's sperm with Emma's eggs in a petri dish advised at their consultation. "You do the math."

Emma pads around the *casa*, nearly tripping over a stray mongrel that lies curled beside Emma's couch. The female dog blinks her weary eyes. Emma lets her return to her siesta instead of shooing her outside. Poor thing needs sanctuary from all those loaded pizzles.

She finds Devon napping naked on the side patio in the dappled shade, soaking up heat like one of the geckos chirping from the walls. He wore no underwear or socks when they met years ago, but these days he even suffers a necktie. A sun bunny misplaced in the Pacific Northwest, he rarely has the opportunity to indulge in carefree nudity.

Emma's forgotten how hirsute he is, with fine, black hair sprinkled across his back, chest, arms, and even his bum. When they first met, still teenagers, his long hair billowed about his head like a nuclear mushroom cloud. Now he cuts it short, controlling its electric mass. She had hoped a baby girl would inherit Devon's wild curls, and swift metabolism—not her muddy hair and heart rate.

Devon's face sprouts a shadow seconds after he shaves, a Brillo pad that chafes Emma's face when they kiss. In college, he shaved designs into the thick beard on his cheeks. Now he wears a close-cropped beard. As he sprawls in the sun, she sees that he'd let his pubic hair grow. Normally he kept the wild bush trimmed so that wiry hairs didn't poke up Emma's nose when she nuzzled his package. Guess he figured there was no point, lately, and let it go *au naturale*.

Emma hadn't been attracted to hairy men, although she'd liked the bohemian look of Devon's out-of-control locks. But his scent had lured her, its potent properties surely linked to his body hair. He wasn't stereotypically good-looking, not overly-attentive, not stylish. He wasn't tall or muscle-bound, more a monkey than an ape. He wore flip flops in winter rain, burped in the elevator, wore out-of-date spectacles that shrouded his eyes. Between the glasses and beard, one could make out little of his face under the black mane. He was odd and oblivious, not at all a coveted Aryan pre-med type, but he left jungle markings in the female dormitories of the tame and moldy Northwest.

Emma was no pheromone slouch, herself. The entire girl's wing followed her menstrual cycle; they all ovulated at the same time.

Boys prowled the hall and were eagerly admitted, but choosing the wrong time of the month got them scratched. Devon suffered Emma's claws more than once before she granted him her estrus cave. She guessed, and feared, that once coupled together, theirs would forever be a shared territory. Once inside, Devon imprinted himself on her sheets, an odor not unlike cooking smells that lingered, not always pleasant, but provoking hunger after satiation. After he left for early morning classes, Emma would cuddle into his pillow, intoxicated by his powerful musk. She couldn't get enough of him.

They couldn't have guessed that with their combined hormonal sparks, like match tips waiting for friction, that they would not be able to conceive a child. It would be years before they made the sad discovery, when they finally decided that the time was right and stopped battling with birth control. And nothing happened.

Her periods continued, as regular as the moon. Then came the basal body temperature monitoring, the carefully orchestrated sex, the abstaining until ovulation to give him a higher sperm count, the chronic missionary position, hiking her butt up onto a pillow to aid the heroic journey of his sperm. Soon sex wasn't about the two of them. Always the phantom of the third, the wanted child, hovered in the room, dictating when they mated. Then the doctors took over, until, finally, conception took place while Emma and Devon were in separate rooms under fluorescent lights. Emma, her thighs and ass bruised from the daily hormone shots, lay spread-eagled for the doctor to retrieve her eggs while Devon hunched over a plastic cup with his dick in his fist (Devonshire cream, he called it in a bad

British accent when their lovemaking was still lighthearted), a humiliating contribution, to be sure. If only most fathers had to be put to this test of commitment first. At home, Devon moved to the couch so as not to disturb her. She was too sore and irritable to miss his smell on the sheets. Lying still on her back and getting up only when her bladder was about to burst, she struggled not to rock the boat as the fertilized eggs inserted into her womb decided whether to evacuate or cling to the life raft of her uterus. To help her pass the time during her required bed rest, Devon made up stories that wouldn't make her laugh. He concocted weird milkshakes and held the glass while she drank through a straw. But he couldn't disguise his doubt, and she can't forgive him his lack of faith—perhaps his misgivings had jinxed them from the start.

Emma stares down at her husband, taking his nude siesta in the sun outside on the palapa. He looks better at thirty-five than twenty. He'd kept a trim figure, adopted contact lenses, tamed his mane. He was not so much quirky anymore, with that defiant desire of youth to be outrageously unique, as he was simply comfortable with himself. Devon never worried about other people's opinions. Even now, a maid or yardman could round the corner and catch his nude snooze. Devon couldn't care less. When was the last time she'd seen him naked? When was the last time sex between them had been about lust? About love and union? Like the Seattle stars that lay so often shrouded behind clouds, she'd lost sight of the fierce attraction that had been the sparkling fabric of their marriage. Their passion burned out in the black hole of sterility.

Devon stirs under her gaze. As always, his cock wakes up first, stretching and seeming to yawn in the sun. Devon rubs his eyes, fists screwed-up like a waking child, and looks up at her. His eyes are green in bright sunlight, with flecks of yellow. In the gray Seattle sky, they're dark and murky, inscrutable. He wiggles his fingers at her to join him on the lounge chair.

"Let's go get smashed." Emma turns back inside.

Devon pads behind her. He sweeps a sombrero off the shelf, places it on his head, clicks his heels together and snaps his fingers. "Olee! Let's go! Hasta la nachos!"

Emma points to his crotch. "Better cover that, instead."

"But, chica, the hat no ees beeg enough," he whines in a nasal accent.

Emma changes into a wrinkled sundress she hasn't worn in years.

"Ay, caramba! Muy bonita señorita!" Devon rubs her arms, looking over her shoulder at her in the mirror. "I forgot you had skin under all those sweaters." He kisses her bare shoulder.

She dreads the lovemaking that Devon no doubt expects. Their vacations had always been about sex, odd since they had no children to escape from. But she craves sun and solace, not passion. She wants a good book and a gentle breeze, not a lover's hot embrace. She feels dry and brittle, like a mummy that disintegrates when exposed to air. Devon would find nothing moist and welcoming about her barren body, her inner planes as uninviting as the vast desert the airplane had chased its shadow across on the flight south.

She would crumble into a pile of ash if Devon attempted to arouse her.

Emma turns in his arms and pecks him on the lips. "Let's get a margarita first." She steps away and into her sandals. "We'll make damn sure the hangover's worse than the food poisoning."

With no itinerary or map, they set off down the beach. Emma normally over-prepares, but this last minute trip left no time for studying travel guides or foreign language dictionaries. At Amanda's offer of her *casa*, they had booked the ticket, thrown their clothes into a suitcase, and made haste to the airport. Here, Emma could recover from the final in-vitro round in warm and fragrant peace. No one could recover anything in the gray and soggy Seattle February they'd left behind, most certainly not sanity. Stepping out into the cold drizzle one recent night and tipping her head back to feel the rain on her face, Emma wanted to drown on the spot like a stupid turkey staring into the watery sky.

The blazing sand burns their tender feet, and they cool them frequently in the surf as they mosey towards town. Emma fills her pockets with beach glass and shells. Two yellow pups argue over a coconut in the surf. A girl changes her bikini top behind a blanket held up by a proprietary-looking boyfriend. A few tourists, obvious by their generous bodies and red skin, mingle with the local families. A motorboat full of passengers without life vests cuts through a pack of body surfers. A fisherman dumps his fresh catch onto the sand. Emma looks away when he unsheathes his knife. Gulls swarm for the castoff parts.

They choose an outdoor table at the first restaurant they come to. Under the shade of a *Corona* umbrella, the waves inch toward their toes. The barefoot waiter looks too young to be out of school, much less earning a living by funneling *cerveza* down thirsty throats. He speaks no English—as they discover most of the locals don't—and they struggle to place their order. Margaritas and nachos, he understands. Emma can't figure out how to request a double, and the boy brings her two drinks. Vendors sell junk hanging from poles across their shoulders, and Emma and Devon repeat, "No, gracias," a dozen times before the food arrives. Emma hands a twenty-peso note—a mere two dollars—to a crone who sells nothing but pity for her poverty.

The server stops frequently in his rounds to observe a surfing competition. One broad-shouldered surfer rides a handstand on his board all the way in to shore. The gentle wave carries him toward the beach as if it is God's palm delivering him to earth. The surfer flips sideways when he reaches shallow water, now standing on his feet with the board on his head. Water streams from his black hair down his face, down bunched shoulder muscles, down his brown belly and yellow swim trunks, down to where his ankles disappear in the white froth of surf and sand. He stands regally. The scattered beach crowd applauds.

"What are the old gods down here? Incan? Mayan?" Emma slings back her drink and crunches ice. "How American that I don't know."

"They worship Lord Quiksilver," Devon says, reading the logo on the surfer's shorts as the man jogs by, heavy board tucked under his arm as though he carries a toothpick. Emma had struggled through the soft sand as though she fought her way *up* a *down* escalator, but his bouncing sprint resembles a stone skimming across the water. Sand sprays from his heels like Mercury's wings. The surfer meets Emma's eyes, and he half bows towards her.

Emma licks salt from the rim of her glass. She makes short order of her margarita, glad she doesn't have to wait for a refill. Devon pushes up her skirt under the table and rests his hand on her knee. Emma tenses.

"Emma?" Devon squeezes.

She refuses to meet his eyes, turning away to watch the water-logged shorts cup the surfer's gluts, hard and round as two bowling balls.

"Emma, what's next?"

"Los toros esta noche," the server says, setting down their bill (which would barely cover a bag of Doritos back home). He makes a riding motion with his hands and pantomimes horns.

"A rodeo's next," Emma says, something else to keep them out of the bedroom.

"That's not—"

"Tonight. With bulls."

Devon's hand retreats as he pays the server. Emma smoothes her skirt.

Emma and Devon catch a ride to the rodeo with the three-generational tourist family vacationing next door. "We don't know how long we'll stay," the matriarch warns. "Carlie—my daughter-in-law—she's pregnant. It depends on the bathrooms. You know how it is."

Locals pack the raised bleachers overlooking the rodeo ring. Climbing up the rickety steps, Emma regrets her sundress. *Careful of Medusa's bush, boys,* she telegraphs to the men below. *She kills millions of sperm at a glance.* The crowd is an undulating sea of bright white, straw cowboy hats purchased at the entrance. Extended families blend into each other. The señoras wear frilly blouses with their pants. Toddlers wander where they please. Jack-in-the-box hands pop out from the dense mash of humanity to prevent unsteady tykes from toppling down the steps. Emma understands that the children in the street earlier weren't untended at all, but were looked after by the entire town. Even without coordinated Baby Gap outfits and personal DVD players in the back of airbag-equipped SUVs, the kids are adored.

Energetic mariachi music fills vast stretches of time between each cowboy's brief attempt to remain seated on bulls angered with painfully-cinched balls. Man and beast battle in an arena stripped of safety. No ambulances, no clowns exist to save these crazy dudes if they fall. The bulls' horns are wrapped to prevent a goring, but if any hooves meet skulls tonight, it's a dark, bumpy ride to the Puerta Vallarta hospital in the backseat of someone's jalopy.

One tired old bull can't be bothered to protest the indignity of trussed-up testicles. He sinks to his front knees in the dirt and refuses to be provoked by the furious, flailing cowboy. Emma hopes the weary beast gets to retire to a field, nuzzling noses with a dried-up dairy cow, but suspects he'll end up on the wrong side of a McDonald's counter.

Devon winces. "Talk about calloused *cojones*."

Couples dance on the edge of the bleachers, heedless of no railing and a twenty-foot drop into the corral. Locked together, their legs press tight into the crotches of their partners as they bounce and sway. While inept handlers prepare the next beast, a white horse dances in the bullring. His rider, a portly man in a sombrero, clutches a *Sol* beer in one hand and the reins in the other, pulling the horse's chin tight to its chest. Its hooves tap out a fast rhythm as if it dances on hot coals. The rider sits still on its back, not spilling a drop of beer. A girl in tight pants climbs down into the ring. She straddles the horse, her back pressed tight to the rider's chest, her butt wedged into his crotch. The horse beats a swift rhythm with their bobbing bodies. Music pulses. Soon another tight-pressed couple bounces on a buckskin horse dancing nearby. The horses tap out a Morse code of desire that transmits up through an orgy of vibrating couples.

Devon flags the potato chip vendor. The cellophane bag crackles as the vendor slits it open with his knife. He sprinkles salt into the bag, squirts in red sauce, presses half a lime over it, and shakes. Emma doubts that's a food-handler's license crinkling in his shirt pocket. She crams thick and crunchy potato slices into her mouth.

Testosterone wafts through the stands like the fetid smell of the jungle surrounding them. Emma imagines wildcat eyes staring down at them through the surrounding growth. She turns to see Devon's eyes glowing at her in the dark. He licks her sticky fingers.

A black rain cloud threatens overhead. A few sprinkles drop, and the fair-weather crowd streams toward the exit, their hats like whitewater flowing downriver. Carlie needs to pee, and it's time to leave.

♥

Emma stands at the edge of the dark water that she hears more than sees. The beach is pitch black and deserted. The ocean announces its advance toward shore with crashing thunder, something ominous in its constant battering of the earth. The sky echoes its boom. Cold raindrops plink on Emma's sun-hot skin. She looks up at the star-dense sky. With little electric city light to steal its shine, the sparkling and vast cosmos spreads out above her. An amber god surfs down the Milky Way—Lord, it's Devon streaking down the beach, his white ass luminous in the starlight.

"Somebody'll see you," she hisses.

He moves close in front of her. He's shorter than she is on the downslope of the beach. His crotch presses against her. The waves tickle his ankles.

"From what I've heard, you don't want to be thrown naked into a Mexican prison."

"Come on, Emma. Let loose. Nobody's around. Besides, I can hardly see you, even this close. We could tell them our clothes got ripped off when we struggled out of the undertow."

"Right, try saying that in Spanish." She backs up to higher, drier ground.

"Guess I'm not like that guy today. That surfer. Mr. Mexican Adonis." Devon steps back, his feet sinking into the softer sand and swirling water. "I saw the way you looked at him. Been a long time since you looked at me like that."

She looks down at him. "I'd understand if you found someone else. Someone younger, who could—"

"Are you out of your mind? You think I'd leave you for some other rabbit? Jesus, do you want me to?"

"Whatever's wrong is with me. We both know that."

"We don't know jack. All those goddamn tests, all that money, and still no clue."

"We've been over all this."

"But you haven't been listening. I'd be happy with a goldfish tank."

"But I wouldn't!"

"You used to be. I don't even know who you are, anymore." He turns around and wades in up to knees.

She starts to turn away, back to the house, but a strangled yelp pulls her back. A rogue wave smacks Devon, knocks him down, grabs him in fists of current, and drags him back to sea.

Just as quickly, before Emma can yell or splash in after him, the ocean spits him back up, *patooey*. Spluttering, he crawls out of the surf. Emma grabs his arm and helps him up to dry ground. He plops his bare fanny on the sand, arms wrapped around his knees, face covered. Emma circles him like a frantic chicken. Without looking, he reaches out and grabs her hand, pulling her down beside him.

"You still blame me."

"I'm sorry. I don't know who I am, either."

She's a baby-crazed monster who can't purchase her own tampons, because the cruel supermarket gods stock feminine hygiene products in the diaper aisle, an emotional landmine Emma avoids. She'd like to go rabid amidst the diapers, shredding Baby Huggies with her teeth and howling to the cruel fluorescent skies. Maybe then she could get the rage out of her system and reconcile herself to the injustice that millions of women had so easily what she couldn't. Maybe then she could go on with her life. But she stuffs the grief down, showing up on time for work and smiling whenever someone asks her, "Why don't you just adopt?" instead of asking these well-meaning mothers, "Why don't *you*?" She despises herself for such pathetic weakness, a twenty-first century woman defining herself by her womb's failure. But she could not be rational about her all-consuming desire to be a mother. She couldn't fight her hormonal hardwiring with reason.

"You're my *wife*. My *lover*. That's who. That's the most important thing. That you're here on the beach with me, to give me a reason not to drown. That we're not alone. It's about what we *have*, not what we *don't* have."

"I know all that up here," she touches her forehead, then her belly, "but not down here."

"How about down here?" He sits beside her and reaches under her skirt. "It's where we started. Can't we start there again?"

She could call him a typical male, call him insensitive, get up and leave. But she understands that sex and communion are two different things and yet the same. She lifts her dress over her head and tosses it aside. She presses herself against his wet skin. She smells him, that intoxicating ripeness of his body mixed with the ocean's salt and seaweed. "This place gets your blood pumping, doesn't it?"

As if she's taken a dunk in cold water, she feels revived by Sayulita's acceptance of reality and its inherent dangers. No complicated legal system casts a tangled web of safety nets. No lifeguards, no life jackets, no rodeo medics, no seatbelts, no minimum age limit, no ambulance chasers because there's probably nobody worth suing. Dogs wander freely without leash laws or neuter clinics, and kids wander without hysterical newscasters warning of escaped pedophiles. It's not a perfect world, she can see that. Her understanding is dim after less than a day here, but there doesn't seem to be a false illusion that life is safe or predictable. In the States, the people operate under the delusion that accidents and illnesses can be prevented, and what's broken can be fixed with persistence and a charge card. When Emma could not get pregnant, it never occurred to her to accept her childlessness or to pray. She had gone to the doctor with the expectation that everything would be put right soon enough. The right medication, the right exercise, the right timing. She had lost any perspective as to when to stop. Always, the solution seemed right around the corner. She had been poked and prodded until she felt like a skewed Picasso canvas. Treatment had altered her beyond recognition. Now what? A future as a dried-up hag with a pet poodle? Surely not, because she's got what no other woman has, and that's Devon. She's not alone, not barren, but a warm, welcoming ocean where he can relax his restless spirit.

Devon had said no, enough. Went down on his knees and gave up, and she'd continued to flail away at him to get up and try again. She'd hated him for his stubborn refusal. How could he know the next treatment wouldn't work? Now she grasps the truth. All along, he'd accepted her as an off-kilter work of beauty, priceless art being damaged beyond repair in attempts to fix it.

Neptune might dislike Devon's flavor, but she suddenly craves him. She wants to pop him into her mouth like sushi, that sea-flavored saltiness lingering on her tongue.

He kisses her. His beard stubble chafes her face. "Sorry. I'll shave."

"I've missed it." She nuzzles her cheek against his.

And then they join like the dogs of Sayulita, knees and palms in the still warm sand, the cool waves of the incoming tide lapping at their heels, the breeze on her breasts and raindrops on his back. Unlike the odd mongrel combinations populating the streets, they are perfectly matched, two puzzle pieces snugging together in a confusing world where very little fits together so perfectly. Her rump is still bruised from the last round of hormone shots, but she welcomes the soreness of Devon pressing into her. The pain brings her alive. She's glad he can't see the bluish skin, or he'd be solicitous and careful. She wants it like this, just two animals without past or future, a necessary and urgent coupling. Raw and simple, the two naïve youngsters they used to be going on instinct and trust. Devon's hand covers hers, and their wedding rings clink.

Later, Devon steps over the stray dog to turn off the bedroom light. They lie in the moonlight that claws its way through the clouds and spills in through the hacienda windows. Emma sees that Devon has three scrapes across his cheek, from his ocean tumble. She also sees that he's shaved a heart in the newly-trimmed pubic hair on his low belly.

"Is that for me?"

"It's been yours all along."

A thought flits through her brain like a butterfly. If ever they were to conceive, it would be in a magical place like this, with steaming fecundity permeating the air. Surely Sayulita would provide the miracle that science could not. Maybe, just like that, her period won't come in two weeks. But she chases the wish away, snapping at its wings. For now it's just the two of them, Emma and Devon, and that's enough. The phantom baby takes heel, and the only third party in the room is the panting dog, curled around her own tail.

Spat, Spud, Spatula, Stud

*T*he couple quarrels on Christmas morning. Boyfriend hands Girlfriend a gaily-wrapped box, from which she pulls yet another gift of lingerie. Girlfriend pokes at the wisp of gossamer cloth and blurts, "Did you try it on first?"

"What're you talking about?" Boyfriend's eager smile slides off his unshaved face.

"So you don't deny it?"

"Christ. If you think I swing that way, then we obviously weren't in the same bed together last night." Boyfriend stomps out.

"It was just a question!" she shouts after him. "Don't get your knickers all twisted!"

She surveys the morning's gift-opening shrapnel, deliberating whether wrapping paper with copious tape qualifies for the recycle bin. Will she contaminate an entire load by her negligent inclusion of adhesive, ruining the goodwill efforts of the entire neighborhood? Or is recycling just a lie to make the citizenry feel good?

She kicks the crumpled newspaper article that sparked their spat. While wrapping presents the previous afternoon with environmentally-friendly newsprint, Girlfriend came across the local liberal weekly's list of *Ten Rules for Boyfriends*. Number one rule: "Don't wear your girlfriend's underwear." A revelation for her, this plague of boyfriends prancing secretly in Victoria's Secret. My God. Boyfriend had chosen ruffled pink pantaloons for the dress-up *The David* refrigerator magnet. Was his choice of doll couture a hint she'd failed to get?

As they'd messed around later on Christmas Eve (she in the scratchy, crotchless panties he'd given her on her last birthday), her mind wandered. Did he buy her these scant unmentionables to wear himself? Which of her ruffles had cupped his package? His schlong in her thong? *No.* As if navigating modern relationships wasn't difficult enough without stocking-swapping to consider. She and Boyfriend haven't even solved the housekeeping-equity problem, and now they must face the challenge of denying Equal Opportunity access to her foundations?

The wadded-up nightie, his well-intentioned gift that caused their rift, crosses its arms, *tsk tsk*-ing her. Despite the domestic disaster—why did she have to ask?—sweet potato casserole still needs to be cooked for his dysfunctional (she's learned to say instead of *fucked up*) family's Christmas dinner potluck. His parents' enthusiastic contribution to urban sprawl elbows its way into the forest fringe, and Boyfriend's mother will complain as usual about coyotes eating her housecats, her wail sailing over the clack-clack of the martini shaker.

"Blend the microwaved sweet potatoes with spices, sprinkle with pecans, then bake. Wahlah! So easy," she had been instructed by sister-in-law, Boyfriend's half-brother's second wife. Mental note: must not slip and call second wife by first wife's name. Remind Boyfriend. Or don't, and let him eat dirt. Serves him right for stretching out her bras.

She pulls the cooked potatoes from the fridge. Efficient, she'd nuked them Christmas Eve while she and Boyfriend fornicated, so she could skip the 'wait to cool before blending' step Christmas morning. The fall-spice smell had drifted into the bedroom, making her hungry. She'd given Boyfriend a rare blowjob. He'd taken his own sweet time in coming, compounding her growing resentment over the panty situation.

Now the chilled, uneasy potatoes clump together, their once inviting aroma sucked into their freon cell overnight. She scrapes viscous potato flesh from shriveled skin and discards the hides. Potato innards shiver nakedly. She plops them into the electric food processor. The high-pitched whirr of the motor drowns out *Silent Night* struggling in from the livingroom stereo. Is there true silence anymore? Always something beeping.

A brown lump (not pretty orange—damn it, sister-in-law meant yams) spins round and round the mixing bowl, chasing its own tail. The spuds skedaddle. The mixing blades can't catch them, managing only to nip them in the butt. Boyfriend professed to love her big hips. Does her generous size merely provide a better fit for him? To think, she had been grappling with vague feminist notions that she should find his gifts of undignified, barely-there garments insulting rather than flattering, when all along he'd lapped her in escaping the gender box.

She transfers the dung-colored mass to the bartending blender. She depresses *Blend*, then *Frappé*. Glop bubbles and burps like molten lava. The partially-massacred potatoes hover above the helicoptering blades. She adds water, wrestles them down, but the bilious clump rises back up as soon as she squashes them. These are cartoon potatoes, animated characters contorting themselves to avoid implements of torture. The blades spin, cutting only air beneath the diminishing potential of the side dish.

She paws through the cupboards, searching for an alternate carbohydrate. She should have volunteered for drinks, everyone grateful as they arrived with a case of Miller Lite and a decent merlot. She curses the city-wide epidemic of grocery stores closed for the holiday. Why does she celebrate Christmas, anyway? No Santa. No God. Even the tree's a fake. She succumbed to the propaganda of plastic being better for the environment. Nothing's clear, not even man and woman. She misses the pine resin smell of the scrappy Douglas firs they used to decorate with tinsel—before it turned out that the shimmering silver was bad for turtles or penguins or some endangered species poster child, or maybe it wasn't tinsel at all, but something else, she can't keep it all straight—as she now misses the hot pumpkin-y scent of the frigid potatoes that huddle in group demonstration, lacking only picket signs to dispute their fate.

Boyfriend lurks in the doorway, shirtless. He surveys the smirking potatoes. "Lemme." He muscles in, confident with tools.

He wrestles the brown muck. The blender spits in his face. He steps back, not willing to admit defeat. He pounds.

"You'll break the blades." Did she *ask* for his help? She passes him a mixing bowl. Of course he thought *she* was the problem. He never believes her. Like with the car that one time. He spills potatoes on the counter as he transfers them. Harder to clean if he doesn't wipe up now, but she zips her lips. At least they're speaking.

He attacks the lumps. The potatoes flail in panic, hoisting their patooties over the side of the bowl. Recaptured, he mashes. His muscles bulge. Sweat drips past his sideburns. The potatoes cannot withstand the assault. They liquefy in terror.

"Watch the chest hair." She picks a wiry strand out of the dish and hands him an apron. Pink. Terrific.

Him in a lace negligee? She snorts.

"See? By hand, the old-fashioned way," he gloats, victorious over the resigned mash. "*Now* back in the food processor." He beats the sludge into submission. The rallying potatoes rise up in one last protest. He forces them down into the spinning blades, quelling the spud revolution.

She says something, but the shrill appliance drowns her out in its epic bid for supremacy over the upstart starch. Silence falls, and Boyfriend scoops the coagulated mess into the baking dish, transforming the glob into a casserole. The pecans she sprinkles look pathetically sparse. Together they spread them out, carefully laying each nut in artful composition. Their heads almost touch as they bow over the dish. She opens the preheated oven, and he slides

84

in the heavy dish. There. They stand with their hands on their hips, gladiators eyeing the oven door as if the conquered potatoes will burst forth, snarling.

The carnal wreckage of Boyfriend's battle splatters the counters and floors, his face and body. She grabs the microwaved sponge, nuked daily to eradicate bacteria. "We need one of those baking mixers. You know, the kind with two metal thingies." She whirls her yellow-gloved fingers in the air to illustrate.

"We used to lick the beaters when Mom made cake."

Children's tongues flicked through metal tines, exploring crevices for pockets of cookie dough or oozing chocolate. "Us, too. Not anymore. Salmonella." She fills the sink with steaming, soapy water. "What'd your mom do with three kids and only two metal thingies?"

"One got the spoon. Dog got the bowl."

"That's disgusting." Didn't his mother ever get to lick the metal thingie? Christ, even the dog got to lick something.

With a look of horror she raises the rubber scraper from the suds. Half the blade is missing, shorn off by the rapacious food processor. The top of the beheaded corpse suffocates somewhere in the casserole.

They meet each other's eyes and laugh, bent over double. She holds the mutilated spatula high. A warrior's spear, emasculated.

She sobers. "What are we going to bring? Top Ramen?"

"Look, it's not a big deal. Just bring the potatoes."

"You've got to be kidding."

"Why not? It's just a piece of plastic."

"You don't understand!" A man wouldn't. Even a man in a peignoir. All future familial relations depend upon her potluck contribution.

"Nobody cares about the food. It's about hanging out."

"Fine." A dagger-point word that means its opposite. "Better bring the spatula with us." She scrubs, making the headless shaft presentable for viewing. "At least they'll know what to look for."

"No way. Don't say anything. Act surprised when someone finds it."

"Someone could choke! That's why they stopped hiding those plastic babies in the Mardi Gras king cakes."

"It's not about choking. It's the *fear* of choking. Lawsuits."

"I told you you're not supposed to stick the spatula in the food processor while it's on."

"Did not. Besides, that's not a spatula. *This* is a spatula." He pulls out the metal egg flipper he repeatedly uses on Teflon pans despite her scolding.

"No, *this* is a spatula." She waves the maimed rubber scraper.

She seizes the dictionary. Both are correct. "What did people do before the invention of the spatula?" she wonders out loud, but what really puzzles her is this: How can the world be understood when even simple words mean different things? How can people make themselves clear? Who knew that a sweet potato was different from a yam? And maybe the columnist was pulling her leg. Hip readers got an in-joke that sailed right over her uncool head. Perhaps the idea of Brad Pitt in Jennifer Aniston's teddy is so preposterous that anyone with a sense of the times knows that it's a dig, and she fell for it like an old-growth log felled by modern machinery. Unless...holy cow, maybe that's the real reason Brad and Jen split.

She rummages for the strainer but can't find it. "We'll just have to find that piece." A daunting, archaeological task.

"Like my mom had to go through the dog's poop when it swallowed a needle."

"Stop. This is the kitchen."

"The vet told her to, so she could tell when it passed. Because if it didn't—"

"I don't want to hear it."

As he continues with details of the excavation, she covers her ears with rubber-protected hands and sings.

"It's un-American to sing the Canadian national anthem," he shouts over her.

"Maybe I'll emigrate." A nation of spitting hockey players would wear plaid boxers or tighty-whities with skid marks. No frilly surprises under their khakis.

"Jesus, how do you even know the words?"

"You know they just changed them?" She had been shocked. More shocked than at televised pictures of civilian executions or rigged Olympics. She thought it took assassinations and war for a national anthem to change, not just polite agreement that one line was repeated too often. She didn't think such quiet compromise was still possible.

The timer rings. Donning the oven mitt, she pulls the casserole from the oven. The spatula scalp glimmers whitely on top of the dense mash. Floating in the mire, an upraised palm.

"No fucking way." Boyfriend nudges it, as if prodding road kill to see if the flattened game twitches.

"What law of physics or chemistry, whatever, caused it to rise to the top?" How will she ever understand the world? She should take a class. Everything changes once she thinks she's gotten it straight.

"A miracle."

Yes. A halo in mud.

Potato guts cling to Boyfriend's bristly eyebrow. He plucks the spatula remains from amidst the soggy pecans and sucks it clean. "Mm." He dips his finger into the dish.

"Don't burn yourself."

He holds out discolored goop for her. "Taste."

She licks his finger. "Mm! Not bad!"

He wipes his hands on the seat of his pants.

"We're late. Better change. Right here, so you don't get that stuff on the carpet."

He strips. His combat gear drops into a gory puddle at his feet. Anxiously pulling on his sweats that morning to see what surprises awaited him, he wore no underwear. Naked, he scratches at his crotch and armpits. Her hand in the insulated glove, she touches his thigh as he leaves the kitchen. The teacup collection rattles on the shelf with his wide-legged stride. She finds oddly endearing the idea of his hairy balls spilling out the sides of her bikini-cut.

Halfway down the hall, he turns. "Did you *want* me to?"

Slake

I watched her drink my beer.

Parked outside, her bike pawed the ground. Her choker matched the Harley's saddle. Wet leather and chrome studs. Behind the bar, a monochrome television weatherman flickered in and out of focus, droning on about the high-pressure region holding our city hostage.

The bartender looked over. "It'll only get hotter." Tattooed flames flickered from beneath his shirtsleeve, licking at his damp and bulging bicep.

She set my empty glass down in its perspiration pool. I signaled for another.

She hooked her boot heel over my footrest. "Not another girly Hefeweizen."

I tried to pay for the fresh pint. The bartender gripped my wrist across the bar. "You're new here."

"It's not your money we want." She drummed her long nails, slippery red, on the foaming glass.

His calloused paw possessed me. "Bet you'll earn a sip."

"Maybe." She wiped my upper lip with her thumb, scratching my cheek. "You're sweating."

I eyed my beer. "I'm thirsty."

She grabbed my hair, pulling my face to her crotch. A denim swatch cut a musky river through her black leather chaps. Body heat trapped in animal hide mixed with desire's loud smell. Her zipper teeth grazed my lips. The jukebox throbbed. Lights flickered. A fan whirred. Footsteps sounded behind me. I waited for a taste as she drank her beer.

Pregnant Pause

*H*e kissed me goodbye, his hand on my Buddha belly. I spanked him, a love tap through his thin suit pants.

The screen door closed between us. He took ginger steps down the driveway. Lately I'd been the one with a peculiar gait, so I savored the switch. He cocked his fanny and reached back to adjust his inseam, for my viewing pleasure as well as to ease his discomfort. He likes putting on a show for me.

He didn't take his chopper despite the clear weather. The bike would be too much after last night, a throbbing memory-enhancer, the vibrating saddle and every pothole a reminder of my deep-seated affection.

Usually he swings himself into the four-by-four in one smooth movement. He inhabits his body with macho grace and ease. But this morning he scooched himself backwards up onto the seat. The sun's glare on the windscreen didn't hide his ecstatic flinch as his keister made contact with the leather. Again, the over-acting was for my benefit. I appreciated the performance. After all, I hadn't gotten to see much of his face last night.

I confess. I'm seven and a half months pregnant. And last night I buggered my husband.

I had trussed up his toolkit in the O-ring he'd purchased at the hardware store for some home repair job he'd never gotten around to, never guessing the consequences of procrastination. I'd had to get the metal band on him quick, he'd gotten hard so fast at the sight of me when he walked in the front door. On myself, I'd strapped a major household appliance we'd never used before, a gag gift that had been good for a laugh, then sank to the bottom of a drawer—a dildo we'd christened "Goliath." I didn't think I'd have the guts to penetrate the man I love with something so monstrously stupendous. Getting the damn thing on with no waistline was a feat of genius; I could see only the whorled-purple tip over the Kilimanjaro of my abdomen. His eyes went wide when he saw the tree trunk sprouting between my hips, rooted in the curlicues of my pubic hair.

Doggie humping him in my gravid state wasn't easy. I struggled not to roll back on my butt like a wobbled Weeble, pulled out of him by the gravitational weight of my beach ball belly and the large mass of my ass, which had expanded as rapidly as my uterus. For leverage, I propped myself up against the bolster purchased for my prenatal yoga course. I wedged the firm pillow against the wall behind me and re-engineered my rear-flank assault. I liked this pose much better than the bladder-strengthening *asanas* we practiced in class; I'd have liked to lift my leg and pee on the teacher's favorite background music if she played those monks humming through their noses one more time. What, can't knocked-up women jam to Nine Inch Nails while they flex their Kegels? Must we be relegated to the bland wonders of Kenny G and his ilk? I know what I'd like do with his goddamned clarinet.

I know. I need to learn to watch my language. My mother-in-law would be appalled, although she'd forgive me for just about anything now that I'm making her a grandmama. But the bun in the oven last night was probably not quite what she had in mind.

My husband had waited out the protracted abstinence of my pregnancy without complaint. I hadn't felt an erotic charge since I started throwing up the day after conception. I couldn't even *see* my bush anymore, much less be in tune with it. No, my resolve to do this was to please him. More of a joke than sex. I needed to connect. To close the distance between us—when we hugged, we had to lean in over my protruding belly to kiss. He'd deprived himself of masturbation, wanting the sympathy pain to bond us. Cut off from our shared sexuality, he was a phantom limb—with a raging itch. Now that I'd scratched his suppressed arousal, inflaming his mind's erotic rash, he wasn't about to give up over minor logistics. He was most accommodating in his movement and positioning.

The power of the fucking unleashed an anger that surprised me. His cock, his sperm, had transformed me, incapacitated me. Made me puke and waddle and swell. Made me bulge in places that had nothing whatsoever to do with procreation; the continental rise going on behind me was off the map. Made me a public artifact, people thinking they had the right to touch my ballooning stomach as if it wasn't my body, as if it wasn't personal and off limits to strangers. Rammed me into a gender-specific role we'd spent our decade of marriage refuting. Trapped me in the inexorable biology of my body despite my having thwarted sexual expectation since saying, "I do." Made me helpless and vulnerable, needing seats on buses, assistance down stairs, and a frigging potty break every three seconds. He had to drive me everywhere now; once we pushed the seat back far enough to accommodate my girth behind the steering wheel, my feet wouldn't touch the pedals.

The thrust of my hard shaft burst through months of pent-up resentment like a pricked, cartoon balloon. I was rough. Not nice. I wielded my cock with no care, taking my hostility out on him. I was the boss, a queen bee with a personal grudge and a wicked stinger. I wanted him to remember this union of bodies for days. Every time he sits, bends, or goes to the john, the searing memory of the sex that created this ache will come back to him with a jolt. As it does to me.

I'm aware that we looked ridiculous. I'm also aware that if the neighbors ever caught sight of us, Child Protective Services would lay rubber as they roared into our cul-de-sac. The authorities would make advance plans to confiscate the baby (we've chosen not to know the gender; there'll be time enough for those expectations later). But we would have been banished from our block's annual potluck years ago if neighbors had peered through our bedroom blinds. They wouldn't understand that this creative intertwining helps ensure that we'll still be together for our child's high school graduation. Some of the old biddies are stopping by for tea this afternoon, to hand out more of the unsolicited advice they've been dishing out to me since my navel announced herself to the world under my blouse hem; one day she's shy and withdrawn, and the next she's a siren heralding what lurks beneath. I toy with the idea of placing the giant's member under a tea cozy next to the scones. "Artificial sweetener, anyone?"

Don't get me wrong. This is a wanted pregnancy, long awaited. Why else would I keep a stick I've peed on as a souvenir of one of the happiest days of my life? So I didn't expect to uncork this much enmity, which I'd hidden even from myself. A dune of spite had built up inside me, keeping us apart as much as the sickness, the fragility, the fear, the doctor's cautions. The fucking eroded the barriers, brought me back to center point like a compass. Just as my physical body was off center, off balance, so was my mind, my perception of myself. I craved a good dose of yang for my yin. I needed his wide-open, vulnerable body splayed beneath me, just as I have been wide open and vulnerable since his invasive sperm rammed my passive egg. I needed him trembling under my thrusts, my catharsis for having surrendered my body to an alien being, stripping me of power. I liberated myself by buckling on a harness.

A vengeful, raw dominance overtook me. The occasional Braxton Hicks contraction I'd experienced lately, my body preparing for labor, was nothing compared to the rocket-takeoff orgasm that hit me out of nowhere. He whimpered when I blasted off from his launch pad, jealous that I allowed myself the searing, keening pleasure I denied him. Not expecting the rush, I toppled backwards like a tipsy sumo.

Did I let him come? Heavens, no. I want to whack his piñata as long as possible before the candy tumbles out. I still haven't let him. I'll make him wait until I'm good and ready and in the mood, when he understands what it's like to invite a tadpole to morph inside you. Whether it's embryo-sized or woman-with-a-weapon-sized, the control is complete. I left him in the bed like a decanted champagne bottle, an excellent vintage. I'm eating for two, so I may as well tease for two.

Besides. He likes it.

I know from the wink, the sheepish grin he flashed me as he backed out of the driveway this morning. His wedding ring glinted in the sun as he waved goodbye. I waved back with placid, matronly affection, my expectant silhouette unmistakable through the screen door. It's been so long since I've seen him so glowing, so radiant…but they say that's what pregnancy will do for you.

The Prince &
the Soda Popper

"**N**o fucking way." The rock star lowered his sunglasses, his first show of interest throughout the parade of look-alikes. Swaggering, dancing, and sneering like him, not one of the body double hopefuls had nicked a reaction from this idle idol. But he perked up for the next contender in the endless stream of mimics. This one looked like he'd stood in line all morning for the wrong audition, dressed for church in worn and ill-fitting corduroy rather than in a Sears version of rebellion like the others. He veered into the room when the casting director stumbled over his name on her clipboard, "Otto Wuh, Www…shit. Otto!" Echo glared down the surreal hallway, packed with nervous impersonators.

"That's me!" Hung heavy to the left, Otto lurched through the door like a side-swiped vehicle that never steers straight after repair. He careened straight into Echo, but his collision-course entrance fractured the rock icon's statue-like indifference.

"Excuse me, sorry, excuse me." Otto righted Echo and dusted her off, swatting her bottom. She swatted him away. He fidgeted and perspired under the bland, fluorescent lights. Echo twisted her skirt back into place, tucked her blouse back into her waistband, and prepared to shoo the impostor back out the door. But the rock star noted the bulge scrunched behind Otto's fly and evolved out of his invertebrate slouch on the casting couch. Echo drummed her manicured fingernails on the clipboard and watched the rock star. Otto stared at the hem of Echo's miniskirt, which she'd hoped would dent the rock star's coma as her runway pivot looped between his couch and the door, but the notorious celeb had remained impassive, moving only once to retouch his pimple eraser. Once the living legend convinced his incoherent generation a decade ago that he knew what they wanted to say, he had nothing further to add.

The rock star's spitting image just stood there, breathing through his mouth. No air guitar or gushing adulation for the snoozing myth. Otto planted his feet wide, knees locked, torso thrust forward, hands wedged in opposite armpits, resembling a goon guarding the stage rather than the modern deity prancing atop it as the masses screamed in worship.

"Christ. Maybe we're long lost twins." The rock star peeled his ass from the seat. His leather pants creaked and groaned, a chorus of bovine commentary about the famous jewels the hide enshrined. The rock star perched the dark glasses on his mop of blonde curls and stood, sliding his hand down low-slung pants to adjust his load.

He inspected the body double up close, breathing in his ear. "Identical."

"Oh, um, no way we could be brothers." Otto spoke to the floor. "Like, you sing, but me, I'm tone deaf." Otto shrugged at the obvious proof of their different gene pools. "Sir."

The rock star circled the body double, red snakeskin boot heels beat-beating a punctuation of scrutiny. He planted himself in front of his twin. "Call me Raj."

"Gosh, I couldn't."

"Think of it as Indian for king instead of my name, if that makes you more comfortable."

"Well, okay, sir, and you can call me Otto, but I don't think that's Indian for anything." Otto's gaze strayed up to the rock star's face, as if he, too, couldn't believe that this was another person and not a mirror. From there his eyes flitted to Echo's hem, then back to the floor, then Raj, then hem, a boomerang gaga.

"Otto. Like the elevator maker?"

"Yeah, I got teased in school."

"A fucking palindrome. Unbelievable."

The body double's mouth moved silently as he furrowed his brow.

"You know, the same backwards and forwards. Otto. Otto." The rock star zipped his heavily ringed finger right, then left. "Mirror image. Like you and me."

Otto's expression brightened. "Gosh!"

Echo exhaled audibly. She tore her gaze away from the rock star and shuffled through her papers. "I don't see your vitae, Mr. Elevator Shaft."

"My vvv…vvv…?"

"Resumé. Credits, appearances. *Et-cet-er-uh*," she enunciated.

"Oh, um, I sorta don't have one." Otto sniffed with a vast upward shift of his left nostril. "Never done anything like this before. My—"

Echo scribbled on her clipboard. "Take off your coat and shirt." The body double hesitated. Echo rolled her eyes. "The ad says the job's semi-nude."

"It's just…the hallway's hot. I'm kinda ripe." Otto sniffed his underarm.

"It's a music video, not a deodorant commercial." Echo clicked her pen.

Otto shed his coat and tie. Damp circles swathed the armpits of his wrinkled shirt. He struggled at his buttons with blunt, trembling fingers. "Sorry. I'm nervous."

"Of course you are. I have that effect on people." The rock star, still in front of Otto, unfastened the shirt, one slow button at a time. Dexterous, long fingers brushed bare skin between the seams as he worked his way from neck to belly. He eased the shirt off Otto's shoulders, meeting his eyes once before he stepped aside, yawning.

"Gee, um, thanks, you—gosh, that's nice of you." Otto shrugged out of the shirt. He swiped the cloth under his arms before tossing it aside and returning to his ill-at-ease stance. Half naked, he shivered. He cleared his throat and studied the floor.

The rock star squeezed the man's biceps, as if testing to see if a mannequin breathed. He breathed in the man's dense, musky smell.

Otto shifted his weight. He looked like the rock star after a concert, dripping perspiration, the shaggy hair at his neck and temples damp. His veins and muscles, taut with tension, pulsed and jumped under thick, red-blonde body hair. He crossed his arms.

The rock star exposed a bare chest under his red leather vest. He squeezed his nipple, chin tucked tight on his clavicle as he inspected the eager nub. He nudged Otto's arms apart and brushed Otto's aureoles. Otto closed his eyes. "They'll need to rouge yours. Look, mine are darker. Plus you'll need one of these." The rock star toyed with his nipple ring.

"I dunno." Otto's head wagged back and forth. "I'm no good with needles."

"Don't worry. I'll hold your hand. You'll need earrings, too." The rock star grasped Otto's shoulders and faced him toward a floor-length mirror. Standing next to each other, they looked back and forth at their reflections. The rock star shed his vest and turned his profile for inspection; his duplicate turned simultaneously. Subtle differences revealed themselves under the hum of the unflattering lights. The body double's farmer's tan spoke of life in the sun, while the rock star was a pale creature of the night. The stand-in packed himself in a dense, corded body, born of activity. The rock star was slim, but no six-pack abs spoke of exertion other than bedroom gymnastics. Clenched jaws and dense eyeliner hardened pretty features, his face locked in the jaws of heavy sideburns. Curled-up fists protested the soft vulnerability of pampered flesh. Heavy jewelry weighed him down, from choker to belt buckle. Dense, red chest hair marked the body double's swing toward Neanderthal, while the rock star's smooth hide exemplified waxed evolution. Their mutual slouches were born of different life stances, the rock star's from ennui, the body double's from self-deprecation.

Their eyes—Raj's green and Otto's blue—met in the rock star's reflection.

Echo looked back and forth between the two. She sighed. "He'll need a wig."

"I've been growing my hair out since I saw the announcement," Otto apologized.

"I'll cut mine," the rock star said.

"We'll call you." Echo pointed to the door. Otto gathered his things and backed out, waving. She slammed the door behind him. "Uncouth."

"Divine," the rock star said to the mirror, picking at navel lint.

"He's got no acting credits. No stunt experience."

"He's the one." He curled his arm and poked at his tattooed bicep.

"You're gonna lay him, aren't you? I wondered why you wanted to sit through a cattle call." She tossed her clipboard aside. "You cooked up this video just for a sex game, huh?"

"Imagine making love to yourself."

"Narcissus died of heartbreak after falling in love with himself." She dropped to her knees between him and the mirror.

"Nobody believes that mythology crap, anymore. Besides, a petty god made Narcissus fall for himself as punishment for his pride. I'm my own god." He inspected his teeth in the mirror, bending over the top of her head. "Not to mention lots of other people's. Christ, watching all those losers today makes it obvious why I'm up here and they're down there. As if they're anything like me. Give me a fucking break."

She unhitched the tarantula belt buckle that dug into his belly, stamping his skin.

"Secondly, lovely Narcissus could only stare at his reflection in a pool of water. Never consummate his desire. Why he didn't masturbate or learn to swim is beyond me, but, point is, I'm smarter than that. *My* reflection will be human, flesh and blood."

"Not smart enough to ask whether he bats for the boys' team." Echo unlaced his fly.

"Doesn't matter. I provide on-the-job training. I hope I'm his first. My proselyte."

"You and your straight boys." She freed his erection.

"They'll give to a god what they'd deny a mere mortal. I merely take the offered cherry upon my altar. Speaking of, listen," he pulled her mouth away, "I'll take a rain check on this, baby." He pushed her away from his wilting woody. The back of her head banged the mirror. He swiped at his smudged mascara. "Maybe tomorrow."

She nodded. "Tomorrow."

♥

Otto took up his posture on the movie set where he'd left off at the audition. His bottle-lightened and permed hair had grown out in the intervening weeks. His shaved chest itched, as did his unshaven face, scruffy between sideburns, but he couldn't move to scratch himself. He stood bare-chested between two makeup artists, his evenly-tanned arms crossed. One on each side of him, the artists clutched a photograph in one hand and a paintbrush in the other, meticulously recreating the rock star's tattoos on Otto's biceps. They worked in a pocket of calm under an awning as cameras, cranes, and sets converged under the California sun. The smell of chlorine cleaved the air as a loud pump chugged water into a giant, makeshift pool.

The rock star approached behind Otto, looking healthier with a bottled tan and boyish in shorter hair. He goosed his twin without warning. "Can't wait to see the one on your ass." The body double started, and both makeup artists cursed, wiping with rags before the paint dried.

Otto blushed. "On my…But I thought this was *semi-*…"

"Sure, it might not show, but it's all about getting in character." The rock star circled in front of Otto, sashaying in his kilt and army boots. "Doncha think?"

The rock star admired the work-in-progress. A colorful peacock spread his tail across one upper arm, a musical eighth note gracing each feather's eye. On the other arm a malefic spider perched on a narcissus blossom. "Tabula rasa," Raj murmured.

"Huh?" Otto checked his fly.

The rock star displaced one of the artists, his hand on Otto's tailbone as he inspected the tattoos. "Why not get a real one?" His finger dipped into the waistband of tattered sweatpants.

"No way, no needles. Besides, Mom'd kill me. Plus I can't sit still. With my job, I'm always on the go. I went crazy hanging out in the backyard trying to even out this tan like they said I had to. Mom said I'd break the lawn chair with all my thrashing around."

The rock star imagined white buttocks sacrificed to the red heat of the sun god. Raj pictured plaid, lawn-chair imprints on damp flesh, sweat dripping onto Otto's comic books, the mound between Otto's legs inflating as he dozed off into erotic dreams—perhaps about the rock star. Bored housewives and closeted husbands gazed down from neighboring windows, the suburbs erupting into a frenzy of masturbation and fornication, as if Eros had shot off arrows from the exhaust pipes of an SUV navigating Otto's cul-de-sac. "What do you do for a living?"

"I stock soda pop machines."

"Hard work. No wonder you're so fit." The rock star smacked Otto's ass again, his hand lingering.

"Oh, yeah. I cart around all those cans, plus I have to move and install the machines, too. Think about where you find most pop dispensers."

"I'm all ears."

"Nooks and crannies. Basements. Under stairways. Around corners. Sometimes you wouldn't believe how I have to maneuver those puppies."

"I'm sure the thirsty of the world thank you."

"I don't get the appreciation you'd think I would. Mostly folks are just mad if their flavor runs out. I don't blame them. I got addicted myself. Had to switch to diet." Otto patted his flat belly. "Don't get me wrong. I like my job."

"I can tell you're good at what you do."

"Conscientious, my boss says."

The rock star turned to the makeup artists, who had taken advantage of the opportunity for a smoke break and to check out the gaggle of goth chicks congregating on the lot's perimeter. They squealed for the rock star, who hadn't glanced their way. He removed his shirt. "How's it looking, boys?" He turned around and pressed his back against the body double's front. The artists returned to their task, working from the live model rather than the photos.

"I, um…" Otto tickled the rock star's ear with his breath. "I wanted to thank you. For choosing me. I know it's not like I have much experience."

"Stick close." The rock star eased back. His kilt-cloaked ass crack snugged against the prize dangling in the body double's sweats. "I'll teach you what you need to know."

"I have something to confess."

The rock star reached back to squeeze Otto's thigh. "I know what you're going to say."

"Then you know I've never heard your music? I'm a country man, myself. I just needed the money for my Mom's—"

Raj pretended that he'd meant to scratch his own leg. "No problem. I prefer it that way."

"Yeah?"

"Sure. This way we can get to know each other, you know, man to man, without all the adulation and worship crap getting in the way."

Echo approached, same skirt, same clipboard. "Shit, is it live or is it Memorex?" Only staring at the two men simultaneously could she pick out their differences. The rock star had unfortunately lost weight, and she knew about something else he'd lost in the weeks since Otto's audition. "Why can't we start filming right away?" Raj had demanded more than once, pouting, pushing away dinner and pushing her away from his limp and unresponsive godhead. Right now his temple column looked eager enough for sacrifice, though, his Hunting Plaid rising in the wind of his passion. Echo, too, had lost weight, her waistband riding low on jutting hipbones. "Why don't you just call him up and ask to see him?" she'd asked, exasperated. "*Please*," Raj had responded. "I can't seem *interested*."

Now Raj shifted his weight from one foot to the other, his wool skirt swaying against Otto's baggy cotton, a friction hula. Otto's swelling package knocked at the rock star's back door as he smiled at Echo over Raj's shoulder.

"Don't let him learn your signature," Echo warned Raj. "Or maybe he still signs with an *X*?" She studied the pair. Despite their physical similarities, a newcomer might pass over the surrogate at first glance, whereas their full throttle stare would stop at the rock star. No matter how hard they tried to ignore his presence, Raj's magnetism would compel their gaze.

Otto peeked at her over the rock star's shoulder. Or perhaps the difference was opposite. The rock star lacked his twin's naïve and pleasing charm. The god remained isolated in his elevation, whereas the mortal was on the invite list to all the tailgaters and backyard barbecues, the vanilla guy who laughs hardest when he's the butt of the joke.

"You need to fast," she commanded Otto, then looked at the rock star. "And you need to start eating. Why don't I make your favorite dinner?"

"Somebody got a mirror?" Raj snapped his fingers. "How're the tattoos coming?"

Echo bit her lip and focused on Otto. "Listen, they're riding my ass for hiring someone with no experience—though once they see you, I'm sure they'll get it—so let's go over this again, okay? It's not rocket science, but here we go. The world is flooded. It's Armageddon or some end of the world crap." The tattoo artists continued to work while Otto absorbed Echo's directions. She used expansive movements, talking loudly, as one tends to shout at the deaf. "There's all these floating grave stones and faces under the water."

"Creepy," Otto nodded.

Echo motioned to the rock star, who watched Otto's face in a hand mirror. "He sees his own name on one of the grave stones."

"But where is he?" Otto looked puzzled.

"He's sitting."

"On what? I thought the world was flooded."

"A fucking flying carpet, for all I care. Jesus. That doesn't concern you. He reaches into the water and pulls you out. And then he sees that it's really himself he's just saved. Only you're dead. So *he's* dead, see? And he's looking down at you, at himself, dead, and he sings, *I had such a fright, I'm chalky white,* yadda yadda yadda. *I'm in peril, I think I'm the devil.* You get the picture. We'll do lots of takes, so we can cut in from any part of the song. All you do is lay there. Just play dead. You're both soaked, and it's raining. We'll make it as comfortable for you as we can, but it won't be a barn party. Then he leans down and kisses you, and right then your eyes open, only it's his eyes."

"We…kiss?"

"So he's brought himself back to life. Then he becomes one body."

"We get the urge to merge!" Raj cackled.

Echo ignored him. "The morphing…" She caught Otto's blank expression. "Him changing into you all happens on the computer later. Don't waste your brain cell worrying about it. We'll get you colored contacts, anyway." Raj's orders.

"Uh huh, to get in character," Otto nodded.

"Whatever. All you do is jump out of water, like he's hoisting you, and play dead. Wait for him to kiss you. Open your eyes. Piece of cake. Got that?"

Otto thought hard. "Well, no, like, why did he split apart in the first place?"

Echo dropped her clipboard. "I'm gonna lose my job."

♥

Raj threw the trailer door open. "Thank God. I was afraid, I mean I thought you'd forgotten to come." He panted, as if he'd leapt for the door handle at Otto's timid knock. He caught his breath and slouched, hooking his ringed fingers in the low waist of leather hip huggers; the flesh-colored pants inched still further down his bony pelvis. "You know, for the costume fitting. Tired of waiting around for you. Got better things to do with my time."

"Sorry. Sorry. I'm real sorry." Otto gazed up at the rock star, perched a few steps up. "Tattoos took way longer than anybody thought." Otto motioned to his biceps. "I'm supposed to keep them uncovered for awhile, 'til they dry real good. I don't think the bus driver'll let me on without a shirt, though."

The rock star yawned and stretched, his bare abdomen bending forwards towards Otto's face. "Let's have a look. Come on in."

"Actually, I was wondering if we could do it tomorrow? Gotta get home. I promised Mom I'd cook—"

"Oh, no. No, no." Raj descended two steps. "It has to be now. I've been waiting so—I mean, we, um, we have to keep on schedule." He morphed his eager expression into stern reprimand. "You want the job, don't you? There's plenty of blokes who'd beg for the chance—" He turned his back, but looked over his shoulder. His ass crack sprouted above his low-riders, making obvious his lack of underwear—though this had already been apparent through the broad lacings of his fly, as a tongue-less sneaker reveals a bare foot.

"Yes, I need the money for Mom's—" Otto took a tentative step up.

"Good." Raj hauled him up the steps and into the trailer and locked the door behind him.

Otto gazed at multiple refracted images of himself in mirrors lining the walls and ceilings. Disappearing into infinity, he couldn't tell which were the rock star and which himself.

"Here, use my cell phone. Have anything your mama wants delivered to her." The rock star's own catered dinner lay untouched behind him. "On second thought, I'll have Echo order it." The rock star snatched the phone back before Otto took hold of it, punched in some numbers, barked out some orders, and hung up. He switched the phone off before setting it down. "Help yourself. Never mind. Here. Sit." The rock star loaded a plate with food and thrust it towards Otto. "Have some wine." He poured a glass to overflowing.

Otto perched on a leopard-print ottoman. "Could I have plastic? I always break those things." He eyed the delicate stem.

Raj sloshed wine into a travel mug. "Eat, eat." He ate up the sight of Otto masticating. He sat opposite Otto, elbows on the table, chin propped in cupped palms. He sighed.

Otto poked at an unidentifiable nibble-sized appetizer before popping the delicacy into his mouth whole. He knit his brows, as if the flavor were a profound puzzle to be solved, then brightened. "Spinach! I like spinach." He popped in two more. Pastry flakes lingered on his lips like dandruff. "You sure this is okay? Ms. Echo said—"

"I wouldn't want you fainting on the set. You've got to keep your strength up. After all, this is your big debut."

"But nobody'll know it's me. I'm supposed to be you."

"And that you are, my friend. Here, try one of these." Raj held a mini-quiche up to Otto's lips. Otto opened his mouth to Raj's insistent pastry-puff prod. The rock star licked his finger. "So, be honest, just between us, did you ever imitate me? Look in the mirror and pretend?"

"Well, no, I was always just me." Otto chewed and wiped his hands on his pants.

"Come on, not even Halloween? Costume parties?"

"I was a fire engine, mostly." Otto slurped wine. "Could I have Sprite in this?"

"You mean, fireman?"

"No. Fire engine. Big red box."

"So people wouldn't look at you and go, 'You look just like the guy on the cover of *Rolling Stone*'?"

Otto shrugged. "Uh uh. Just me. Nothing special."

"No shit, you never thought about changing shoes with me? Just for a day? Dress like me and see if you could get some ass?"

"Gee, then who would do my soda route?"

"Have another oyster." Raj shoved a mollusk in Otto's mouth. He drained his wine glass and stood, unlacing his fly.

Otto looked away as the rock star stripped beside him. "I had to bribe my cousin to cover my route while I—" The rock star's nude form, front and back, ricocheted back to him from the mirrors no matter where he looked. He stared at his plate, apparently ruminating on his brie.

Raj stepped out of his pants and thrust them at Otto, his woody rising in the vicinity of Otto's left ear. He stroked his erection a few times, as a mere mortal might unconsciously pick at a scab. "See if they fit."

Otto scanned the room. "Where's the can?"

"Don't be shy. You're an actor now. The body is but an instrument. Like a guitar."

"Or a piano?"

"Sure, a piano."

Otto stood and turned away, stepping out of his sweats and into the leather pants.

"Uh uh. Tighty-whities, too. No unsightly panty lines."

Otto hesitated, then removed his jockeys.

"Hang on. The laces'll catch your pubes, never mind how Gucci caveman you'd look." Still naked, Raj fetched shaving cream and a razor.

Otto held the leather pants over his groin. "No way you're shaving my beanie wienies."

"It's better if someone does it for you. Less chance of nicks. That's why I choose waxing. Now unleash the beast. Wow. Christ. We're not identical, after all. Jesus. Good thing we're not shooting a nude scene. I'd be laughed off the set. Go ahead, look. Forget that locker room crap."

They turned to the mirror and looked back and forth, Otto with furtive glances and the rock star with an undisguised stare, comparing tools as if choosing a wrench in the hardware store. Mirrors multiplied their love poles exponentially around them. The rock star's jewels were nothing to be ashamed of. Just average. But one expects more on a god than dimestore baubles. The body double's salami, however, was the stuff of legend. His unaroused member, densely forested, dwarfed the rock star's hard-on sprouting from a clear-cut.

Raj faltered. "You know the ancient gods had tiny pricks? Zeus had a Lilliputian lightning bolt between his legs. A shrimp dink. Maybe that's why those Greek heroes liked boys. Only ones they could impress. Now, today, if we decorated our soda cans like they painted their pottery, it'd be you parading around the side and not me. Not that you'd fit."

"No way. Besides, no more posing for me after this. All this handling's getting under my skin. I feel like one of my pop machines."

"What would come out if I inserted payment and pressed the right buttons?" Without waiting for an answer, Raj dropped to his knees and lathered Otto's meat, as if he couldn't wait to get his hands near this magnificent member.

"I'm a piano. Piano. Piano." Otto whistled at the ceiling.

"Hold it up, would ya?"

Otto seemed relieved for the excuse to grab his organ, which cowered with the proximity of the miniature lawn mower in Raj's hands. Raj worked slowly and carefully, his face close to Otto's crotch. Sweat dripped down Otto's body. Finished, Raj wiped away the shaving cream.

"Um, I think you've got it all."

"Almost done." Raj stroked a damp cloth between Otto's legs. "Okay. Try those on, now. Let's see how they fit."

Otto wiggled into the snug leather pants. He struggled with the laces, which had come loose from the eyeholes.

"Here, let me." Raj re-threaded the cord, criss-crossing it over Otto's exposed groin. "I have to tie it from behind, though, like I'm used to." Raj stood close against his twin's back and reached around him. "Hang right. Believe me, somebody'll notice if we're hanging on different sides. And I always hang right. It's well-documented in certain chat rooms." He reached into the body double's pants leg and re-positioned Otto's pecker. He held on longer than necessary. "Hmm, a little tight. You okay with that, or you want them to let the seam out a little?" When he removed his lingering fingers, he'd lost two rings.

"No, it's…that is…it'll be okay if I'm not, you know…"

"You've got it backwards. The harder you are, the better. Believe me, they'll stick a sock down there if you aren't. Of course, the way you walk your dick, it might be hard to tell." Raj pulled the laces tight with a vicious tug, but the pants still gaped open, their circumference too small for Otto's butt and basket. "Tomorrow we have to kiss, you know."

"Yeah, I'm a little nervous about that. I was kind of awake all night worrying about it."

Raj imagined damp and twisted sheets. "Just lay there. I'll do everything."

"Yeah?" Otto turned around, tugging at the seat of his pants.

"It's no big deal. Tell you what. I'm pretty busy, but let's practice now while no one's watching, so you'll be more comfortable tomorrow."

Otto opened his mouth to protest, and Raj promptly inserted his tongue, his nude body smashed against Otto's, hands grappling with the laces.

Otto twisted away. He banged his head against a mirror, eyes wide. "I, I think I got it."

"Did you feel it, too?"

"Well, that snack did upset my tummy."

"Have your way with me." Raj spread his arms. "I'll allow it."

"You mean—?"

"I know you've been wanting my body. Everybody does. You're just too polite to ask. I love that about you. So humble." Raj stepped towards him. "Fuck me now."

"Oh, boy, wouldn't that, um, hurt?" Otto backed away.

"You're hung like a yak, I'll hand you that, but don't worry about me. I've taken freight trains up the ass." Raj continued his advance.

"I really should be getting home. Mom's wai—"

"I'll pay you."

"Sir, you already doubled my salary."

"I understand your hesitation. Someone like you making love to someone like me seems *impossible*, I know. Your mind must be having trouble fathoming your luck." Raj dropped to his knees and grasped Otto's calf. His voice climbed half an octave. "Then just let me watch you come. Handle your meat like you're alone. I won't touch. I just want to watch. I—I can never keep my eyes open when I do it myself. I want to see what I, what you, look like." Raj rose up on his knees and pawed at him. "Come all over me!"

Otto checked his Pooh watch. "I can just make my bus!"

Raj grabbed his arm. "Use my limo. Use me. I'll go with you!"

Otto pulled away. "But I support public transportation." He backed out the door.

"What about dessert?" Raj wailed.

Otto fled the trailer, bowling Echo over as she reached up to knock. He set her back on her feet and dusted her off, catching her glare as he brushed her bosoms. She eyed his gaping pants. "Having fun?" She smoothed her skirt.

"These are, um, we were trying on outfits."

"I'll bet. You're hulking out of those, sweetheart. I'd suggest you try the costume shop tomorrow instead of Raj's closet."

She left him stammering and found Raj naked on his knees in the trailer, licking Otto's plate. "Well, at least you're eating. Or is that just a supplement to a recent protein diet?" She paused. "I don't believe it. You haven't seduced him, yet? It's been nearly twelve hours."

"You can't rush these things, you know." Raj mouthed the rim of Otto's cup.

"That's never stopped you before."

"This one's different."

"I see something else that's changed. Hello, stranger." She eyed his yearning erection as he crawled over to Otto's heap of clothing and smelled his underwear. "Those pants you packed him into aren't going to work, by the way."

"I agree. I think the kilt." Raj pictured the skirt flying up as Otto leapt into his arms from the turbulent waters of desire.

"Oh, really. Why not naked?" she drawled.

Raj nodded. "You're right! The side of myself that I pull free should be unadorned. Spiritually pure! Psychically cleansed!"

"It was a joke." She knelt next to him. "Perhaps I could relieve you of that—"

Raj grabbed Otto's jockeys to his crotch, blocking her reach, then groaned. His exhalation fogged the mirror in front of him. He opened his eyes. "Too late."

"Premature, not late," she sighed.

♥

Echo pulled Otto aside as he dried off between takes. "We need to talk."

Otto tugged at the wet kilt plastered to his thighs, trying not to stare at the water splashes on her silk blouse. His sides were bruised from his constant leaps onto the blunt edges of the fake cloud Raj danced upon. His fingers and toes were pruned from his long day in the pool. Raj kept flubbing his miming when he grasped Otto's hand and pulled him from the water, so the kiss scene hadn't been filmed after a week of shooting. Otto had avoided Raj's trailer, and it looked to some as if Raj were trying to cop a feel under Otto's skirt whenever the stunt double jumped from the pool.

"Listen, Otto, I'll give it to you straight."

"I messed up, didn't I?" Otto grasped her hand. "I swear I'll do better next time."

"It's not you. It's Raj. He's not looking too good on camera. No, you, you..." Her eyes swept up and down his near-naked form. She blinked. "You look just fine. But Raj isn't performing well.

118

He's starved for…His rings keep falling off." In the distance behind them, Raj hung dejected over the side of his cumulus puff, staring hangdog into the pool while the director paddled out on her skiff to lecture him. Echo lowered her voice. "He's wearing a fake butt and an over-ripe zucchini under that tartan. He's fading away."

"Does he take his vitamins? I take my multi every morning with my Cheerios, and I never get sick."

"This is *love* sickness, Otto. Surely you know what that feels like." Echo looked away, her eyes wet.

"Are you okay, Miss Echo? You look like you could use a ham sandwich, yourself. I make a terrific mac and cheese with tuna—"

Echo sniffed and snarled, "I'm fine. But he's pining away for you." She fingered the safety pin holding up her sagging skirt.

"He did mention something about a caboose." Otto scuffed his wrinkled toe into the dirt.

"We've got millions riding on this project. We should have wrapped days ago. Look, we need you to take one for the team. *Capiche? Comprende?* Unnerstand?"

"Aw, I don't know. I mean, if it was *you*—" He tried to smooth down the front of his rising kilt.

"If it was me, I'd screw him in a heartbeat. Are you kidding? Do you know how lucky you are that he wants in your pants?"

"I meant—"

"We'll make it worth your while. Monetarily."

"He said the same thing. Do I look so, so—"

"Gay?"

"No, poor." His kilt sagged. "So you knew he was AC/DC? Like all those gods he talks about?"

"Pansexual, you mean. Welcome to the twenty-first century. So what do you say?"

"I wish I'd never left my soda route. I never had problems like this. I mean, there was this one guy who rubbed my butt once, but I just thought he was nearsighted and meant to push the orangeade button. It's all so complicated, now."

Echo noticed his high beams. "How's that nipple ring healing?" She reached out, but stopped herself from touching the silver hoop.

"Fine. Sorry again about fainting."

"No problem. Your having a real one adds to the authenticity. We appreciate your willingness to rise to the occasion."

Otto's half-mast flag climbed again to his internal anthem. He swatted at the plaid wool. "Yes, a real one helps."

"Water too cold for you?"

Otto shivered under her stare and shook his head.

"No, it certainly doesn't look like it's dampened your enthusiasm." She chewed her pen. "For the project. Listen, Raj has to go to a press conference. He needs to work a miracle. Sales have plummeted. Why don't you take a hot shower in his trailer?"

"So I can wait for him, you mean?" Otto hung his head.

"Yes. Yes, so you can wait for him."

"If that's what you want, Ms. Echo, I'll do it. For you. But no money."

♥

120

Otto leapt up at the knock on the trailer door. Echo poked her head in. Otto threw down the supermodel calendar he'd been thumbing. "I was just, um, checking to see if Mother's Day was coming up."

"Somehow I believe you."

"Anyway, he's not here. Still at the press conference." He eyed her breasts, then batted at the damp towel hooked around his waist, as if beating at an insect.

"I know." Echo stepped inside and locked the door behind her. "I thought I could help prep you." She lifted his towel. "My god, you're *not* identical."

"Oh, man. Oh, geez." Otto stepped back, bumping a mirror.

Echo dropped to her knees. "I'll do anything you like. Just pretend you're him." Her head disappeared under his towel.

The mirror behind Otto shrieked as his towel rode up and his damp ass skidded across the glass. "Wow, hello? Down there? You sure you're okay? You're so thin. I've been worried that you're sick." Otto spoke between gasps. He planted his feet wide for leverage against her insistence. "Maybe you should be home eating chicken soup instead of working so hard."

Echo poked her head out. "Me? You're really worried about me?" She ducked back under the damp fabric's mantle.

"Oh. *Oh. Oh!* OhmanohmanohmanohGOD! Stop!" Otto pulled her head away. He bent over double, grimacing. His Johnnie jumped under the towel like a cat caught under the bedsheet. "Geez, I almost came in your mouth."

"That quick?" Echo wiped her smudged lips.

"Well, um, I'm not too good with girls," he panted. "It's been, well, awhile. And you sort of know what you're doing. I'd say."

"You care that you'd come in my mouth?" Echo sat back on her haunches.

"Well, yeah…I'd rather…gosh you're beautiful." He pulled her to her feet. "Can I—I want to make love to you. Golly, you're gorgeous. Like a, a, a nymph or something. Think he's got rubbers?"

"He never thinks about stuff like that. Thinks he's immortal."

"Then let me just kiss you." He fondled her breasts.

"Are you *serious*? Just *kiss*?"

"With you it'd be enough. Although I definitely want to, I mean, *goshIwantyousobad*." He smashed his face against hers. His rough hands traveled everywhere, down her skirt in back, up her skirt in front, tearing at her blouse and her bra. Something somewhere ripped. He lifted her and lay her back on the bed's red satin sheets, shredding her pantyhose, and planted his face on her mound. He munched away. His enthusiasm rocked the trailer.

Echo thrashed and groaned. "You're definitely *not* related to him," she cried.

Echo came and came and came, her moans bouncing off the glass walls. She blinked down at him. "What an ass I've been." She lay back, panting, and lit a cigarette. "You know his name is really Roger. Raj for short. And you, I think you're really Auto Pilot." Her smoke ring floated up to the mirrored ceiling, crowning Otto's divine lingam before fading away. She noted his unfailing hard-on as he lay beside her, an ass-happy grin splitting his slick face.

"Look, I'm on the pill, and I'm safe. I've done nothing but give him blow jobs for months, and he hasn't managed even that since your audition."

"Well, I, I, I, I'm definitely safe, too. I, um, I've, uh, never done it."

"Never? At your age? You mean a *virgin*?"

"I hate that word."

"You'll never have to use it again after today, sugar."

"Just, promise me—that you're with *me* right now, and not with *him*."

She folded the towel back over his chest like a bridal veil and climbed on top of him. "Baby, does it feel like I'm with him?" She lowered herself onto his Corinthian column, and he erupted like Mount Vesuvius belching after swallowing a virgin sacrifice.

♥

Echo ached. She dripped and throbbed. She'd lost track of positions and numbers, but, asleep beside her, Otto threw another woody. He scratched at his shaved teabags and passed gas. They both were streaked with crusted passion. His ass was red as the sheets from her claws and spanks. He was a ready and able learner, as quick in the bedroom as he had been in front of the camera. His peacock and spider tattoos were now colored smudges, like bruises.

Echo reached for the rest of the grilled cheese sandwich Otto had fixed for her mid-coitus, alarmed at her jutting hipbones.

The doorknob turned just as a flash lit up the room. Echo peered out the window as a crack of lightning retreated into the otherwise clear sky—no one stood on the trailer's step. She cried out at the bolt's nearness and curled close to her lover.

Otto reached out for her and held her tight. "Raj back yet?" he mumbled.

Echo reached between his legs and captured his electric rod in her fist. "Don't worry about him. He's probably out getting blasted at the bar, cooking up some trap for you." Smoke tendrils curled up from her fire-starting friction.

When they stepped outside the following morning on the way to meet Otto's mother, a narcissus blossom, white petals clustered around a gold stamen, wilted atop a pile of ashes on the trailer's stoop. A peacock shrieked and pranced away as an arachnid polished her paws over the flower's dewy nectar. Otto burst into song, his newfound melody as pure as Orpheus's delicate notes floating down the river Styx, where Narcissus still gazes upon his own reflection.

Not Suitable for Children

So why don't you just adopt? my friends all want to know, crossing their legs and wincing when I tell them about the latest procedure. After all, it would be the politically correct thing to do. Bring back an orphan from a third-world country and parade the wide-eyed infant around as proof that I really am the wonderful person they know me to be, not this medical-technology-crazed, bio-clock-obsessed slave of my ovaries and basal body temperature.

Don't you remember the *Bob Newhart* television episode? I say. The one where the adoption agent inspects Bob and Emily's apartment, and Bob has to say in that stuttering way of his that he's willing to give up his private study for a nursery?

Give up my study? Where am I supposed to go for peace when my husband starts singing, "Please don't fiddle with the Oreo middle," or revs up to the Fig Newton climax, complete with one-legged, flamingo-stance finale?

And, really, who's to determine the square footage necessary for a creature the size of my cat? Is there a formula I missed while I slept through high school trig? Let's get real, here. A kid could fit in my sock drawer and not know the difference. Don't we, as parents, get to determine when he's ready to sleep apart from us, like when he gets his college diploma, maybe?

Okay, I'm with Bob; I'd give up my room tomorrow if someone left a swaddled child on my doorstep, clutching one of those mysterious monogrammed lockets with a daguerreotype of a melancholy woman inside, or half a perfumed handkerchief with the surname initial torn off. But I have never understood how the Newharts managed to be calm while that agent determined whether they were feasible parents. Invite someone into my home to decide whether I'm worthy enough to take in someone else's unwanted children? Our house isn't even big enough to inspect, for heaven's sake. We would have to buy a new 3-bedroom, 1.5 bath with security system, fenced yard, and attached three-car garage (complete with mini-van equipped with air bags) at the end of a cul-de-sac before filling out the application. And put up happy family pictures in the kitchen instead of the watercolor of fornicating carrots.

And what would the inspector say about my bookshelf, with the de Sade biography and the obvious penchant for Anaïs Nin? The tarot deck and the "Story of O?" I know that sculpture looks like an erect, larger-than-life (more's the pity) phallus, but, trust me on this one, it's priceless art with spiritual significance. Would you like me to smash it?

Or our dresser? Would he paw through the underwear compartment? Find the crotchless panties? Discover the sex-toy drawer, the one we're always afraid the dog sitter is going to get into? I mean, if the official has problems with the lack of nursery space and Nabokov, what on earth would Herr Comrade think about the vibrator in the shape of an over-sized, pink plastic lipstick, stored with extra batteries? Or the double-ended dildo we got while high in Amsterdam, which he'd point at us in two-pronged accusation? So what if we've never actually used it? Trying it on in the tiny dressing room with the assistance of the six foot three, mini-skirted, Dutch beauty is about as gymnastic and kinky as I'll ever get. As if the agent would believe that, pacing around our house in his black, ankle-length, opera coat, impatient because we've interrupted him on his way to a twentieth anniversary occasion with his wife, mother of his seven blonde children, all boys, who sing in the choir and know the Boy Scout motto by heart. And, fuck—oops, guess I'd have to learn not to swear.

He asks us what we do for a living. He's trying to catch us out in a lie, because we've got all of that written down on two feet of forms, the carbon quadruplicate kind where you have to throw the whole thing away if you make a typo.

My husband, who's cut off his beautiful ponytail for this interview, answers that he finds employment for people on the county's sexual deviancy list, and I murmur and cough that I earn money as a secretary, but that if we had a child I would stay home and earn extra pennies writing about the pleasant adoption experience and how fulfilling and complete my life is now. I would

127

publish my piece on tending roses without environment-damaging chemicals, blasting off aphids every morning with the hose like a Martian ray gun. Woo! It's a satisfying and harmless way to release latent aggression. Of course I would never employ this method during water rationing periods. I lay my hand on my heart as I smile at him, but he doesn't smile back, and I can't make out his eyes behind the mirrored sunglasses.

He asks me what else I write. His questions have no question marks, so screw Strunk and White when you're dealing with the caretakers of orphans.

Do I have to tell him about that really dark period when I wrote explicit and deviant smut? But I got it out of my system, yes I did, though my husband and I had really hot sex while I was writing it, and he wishes I would write some more. I can't get myself to throw the stuff away, because some day I just might write that best-seller, yes, I will, and Oprah will select me, and then they'll publish my underground erotica the way they did Anne Rice and Anaïs Nin: Jennifer Dawn Munro, writing as J. D. Shaft. The erotica will actually be the stuff that makes my name, that catapults me onto college class lists and into feminist conferences. I already know what I'm going to wear to the conference, you know that butchy pair of black slacks and wide leather belt with the heavy silver buckle? If I can still fit into them, that is. All of this stress makes me binge eat my chocolate-flavored soft calcium chews.

Even if I don't confess this phase to the agent, it's there on the shelf where he'll find it when he goes through my personal journals to prove that I have a poor relationship with my mother and lust after my father, no, that I have a poor relationship with my father and lust after my mother. There's no mistaking the subject matter with the title of my masterpiece, my porn-manners treatise, "Pride and Penetration."

Then he'll find the final incriminating piece of evidence, the bathrobe stolen from the Love Motel in Japan, the building with the quarter-scale Statue of Liberty replica on top. I lost my virginity there with an American sailor, and we overflowed the bath water onto the floor with the weight of our bodies. This moldy bathrobe is all that remains of that day. The agent shakes it at me. "If you had really repented, if you were decent, you would have mailed this back!" My husband didn't know I still had that, so there goes my marriage as well as my hope of imitation procreation. How could I possibly explain to this inspector the remembrance of the pair of us sneaking down the back stairs of the motel, giggles smothered in the stolen robes? How that boy had sailed off to the Persian Gulf, been kicked out dishonorably because of alcoholism, and I had never seen him again? That he was a Catholic and probably had dozens of children by now, and, hell, maybe *he* could spare me one, could you track him down, maybe? But the inspector won't let me evade the question, "Did you? *Did* you?" He shakes the bathrobe with the upraised hand and torch monogram on the breast pocket. "No," I cry, "we didn't use condoms!" and all is lost. I can see what he's thinking: "No wonder God didn't want you to have children."

Why must I explain that all I have is this bathrobe to remind me of what I once was, of what that boy, what we, could have been? What form, what check-marked box, what inspection could indicate that this was about innocence and joy, about hope and love? What carbon copy can explain the deeper love I have for my husband, love that comes with age, and which a child would forever bond? What application can determine what I deserve? What anybody deserves? It's not like a Home Equity Loan or the GRE, for crying out loud. How many people would pre-qualify for parenthood? What form could have foretold that Nancy the prostitute would care for street urchin Oliver Twist?

Take my friend, who, late in her pregnancy while painting the nursery (with toxic paint, I'm sure) got an itch up her butt and scrawled obscene graffiti in baby blue all over the walls. Nobody stamped "denied" on her application and enforced an evacuation.

Do sperm, having passed an entrance exam, queue up at a border crossing checkpoint, scanning a dossier on parental pre-quals they are handed like programs you get from blue-haired ladies at the opera? The mustachioed tadpole licks his finger, or perhaps wears one of those little rubber finger caps, as he thumbs through the stack, flipping back to check a cross-reference, humming as he concentrates. He comes to a locked-brake halt. "You watch hockey?" He closes the dossier and executes a spectacular suicide dive out of the queue. The next tadpole takes his place. "You have overdue library books?" The judges award his dive an 8.6. On they march. "You snuck a grape in the produce department?" The last tadpole, handed the dossier, sighs. "You're addicted to *Masterpiece Theatre* but don't pledge to public television?" His dive earns the gold.

No. The only test biological moms have to pass is being able to direct a urine stream onto a thin stick (the things they never teach you in college). This little wand of hope turns blue if she's aimed correctly, if her husband has aimed correctly, and if the sperm has practiced his laps, managing to swim up the correct channel and hang on like one of those burrs that stick to your pants cuff while hiking; no amount of shaking will dislodge the tenacious bugger, and no matter how many times you think you've picked it off, it shows up again on an errant sock or between your sheets in the middle of the night.

I snatch the cheap terry robe from the agent's Nosferatu fingers and hold it to my breast. No, no, no, I won't rip it up, and where the hell *was* that, anyway? I've been looking everywhere for it.

Adopt? I would be arrested when he publishes his findings in the Ballard News Tribune! I would be publicly displayed as a bad example by intolerant extremists, stripped naked and humiliated by cellulite. Of course, there's no such thing as bad publicity, and my embarrassing fifteen minutes might win me a book contract.

Try to explain to him that not all motorcyclists are Hell's Angels, that we really are going to take the rusted lawnmower in the yard to the dump, and damned if I know how our dog manages to get a hard-on even though he's been fixed for years. I boot him out the door, the adoption agent I mean, not the dog, bellowing, "Get out! Get out! Get out!" I turn to the dog. "Put that disgusting thing away!"

Adopt! You must be out of your minds!

Doghouse

*S*he catches her boyfriend's scent in her territory. He's left his mark: biscuit crumbs on her laptop. Hunting drop-down menus, she stalks his tracks. She pursues his foraging file pathways, chasing his cookies. Her nails scratch as she double clicks. Her mouse sniffs out the end of his trail. A tame-sounding site. She pounces. Expecting to flush out a fairy tale, beauties under beasts beset her instead.

He pads home from work, hangdog tired, tail tucked, hounded by deadlines.

She traps him. Pixels betray his lust for game sport.

Outfoxed. Ensnared by the Net, a nasty byte, he paws at Escape. He bares his canines, at bay. She's got him cornered. She'll go for the kill.

But she doesn't attack. "Arf arf." She grabs his necktie. "Time to walk the dog."

His hush-puppy eyes go wild as she tightens his collar. He licks his chops. She frees his bone. He points, dead set. He pants.

"Bad boy," she growls. "Not housebroken, yet. *Down.*"

The Erotica Writer's Husband

*T*he erotica writer's husband bangs open the front door and stomps outside. Barefoot, with his fly half open, he'd interrupted his current activity when he heard barks and feline screeches.

His wife's cat, puffed up to dramatic size, hisses from the safety of the yellow window box. Marigolds splash against bristling black fur. Fastening the buttons of his 501s, the sex author's spouse scans the yard for the offending dog, but the husband's eyes meet the neighbor's, instead.

"Sorry!" The neighbor snaps a leash onto the collar of his now slash-nosed and cowering mutt. He notes the open-flied jeans of the erotica writer's husband. "Oh *hoh*, your wife must be home. I bet you spend a lot of time with your pants down, being married to a porn writer and all. Doing *research*."

"Uh huh. Well. Gotta get back. She's waiting."

"Don't let me keep you!"

The sex author's spouse waves and carries the angry cat inside. The cat rakes his wrist in one final protest and leaps free. But instead of returning to the slick and sprawled wife his neighbor imagines, pen tucked behind her ear to take notes as she commands him to enact tawdry scenarios, he returns to the john to finish his interrupted piss.

His buddies and neighbors, jealous of a man married to a scribbler of lewd tales, imagine his rampant and orgiastic sex life. His wife is obsessed with sex manuals and adult websites, they think, not home décor catalogs like theirs.

In fact, as husband to a smutty authoress, he suspects that he's getting less than they are. He doesn't know whether to dissuade them from their faulty beliefs in order to gain their sympathy or to continue to bask in the glow of their misplaced admiration. After all, they think he'd been stud muffin enough to capture a lusty wench in matrimony, whereas they had landed frumpy *frau*s more interested in dozing than dildos. There were worse things a guy's friends could assume. They'd given him unsolicited and unearned respect, rarely seen by a monogamous, suburban man with no aptitude for sports. How empty would their lives be if they no longer had his prowess to worship? Who was he to disappoint them by correcting their misapprehension?

As he contemplates the remote control or a nap, the erotica writer herself cracks open her study door. Her laser printer huffs in the background, expending more energy over sex than husband and wife have in the past month. "Everything okay?" she asks.

"Just Dufus Rufus chasing Frizbeehead again. She scratched me." He holds out his clawed arm.

"Better sterilize that. Antiseptic's in the bathroom cabinet. Oh, mind doing the dishes? I've got this deadline."

"Sure, hon. Listen, can we talk, I—"

"Damn, now I've forgotten that perfect word. Shit, I spent the last half hour with a thesaurus and now…stupid dog. Somebody needs to put him out of our misery." She scoops the cat up and closes the door.

He wishes she would spend a half hour with her finger in something other than a book.

♥

That evening he suggests that they might spend some time together, since it's the weekend, but she encourages him to go watch the game with his pals. "Go out and have some fun. Becky's giving me her feedback on that story I've been working on."

"The slaves in the ice castle one? In Greenland?"

"Not Greenland. A hidden fjord in Svalbard. No, I couldn't figure out how the characters could stay warm enough to be turned on. I got cold just thinking about it. Now they're on a boat. Only the Master goes ashore, but that gives the favorite slave time to secretly practice his violin. But of course someone hears him playing the *Paganini Caprice No. 24* and finds him, and then he has to decide whether he wants to stay willingly."

"Still working the gay market? I thought you'd had it with all that spunk." He knows better than anyone that both the dentist and doctor have documented her strong gag reflex, which precludes certain bedroom activities.

"Pays better, and you said yourself the truck transmission's about to go. Anyway, the slave's going to have a *guiche*, so I need to do some research before Becky gets here."

"I know how to make quiche."

"A *guiche*. Not quiche. A piercing *down there*."

"Ouch."

"Then I'm hitting the hay early so I can get up to do my edits. Mind sleeping on the couch when you get home so you don't wake me up?"

"How about we roll in the hay instead of hitting it?"

"Funny man. I married you for your sense of humor."

♥

He receives an ovation when he arrives at the bar. His friends clear a stool for him.

"Have a beer!" Dean cries. "You must be exhausted!"

"Drink up!" Doug says. "Replenish those fluids!"

"Do a shot, man," Dave advises. "You can't spare the time for a pint! Gotta get back to the little wife!"

They check their watches. "How long you need to regenerate, man? We'll let you know when time's up."

His cell phone rings. "It's my wife. I better pick up."

"Time for dessert!" They all jeer. "Second helpings!"

"Mind picking up some buttermilk on your way home?" his wife asks. "I'm making bread tomorrow."

"Sure, hon." He wishes she would knead something other than flour. The only thing rising in his house is dough. They could milk his meat, instead. Beat his eggs. Eat her jelly roll. Toss his nuts. Warm her bread basket. Hot cross his buns. Make baby batter.

"So, what'd she want? Come on, you can tell us."

"Lovin' in her oven."

They whoop and slap him on the back. His Hefeweizen splashes his shirt.

"Come on, spill the beans, man. You never tell us anything."

He swipes at his soggy shirt, imagining:

He bangs the front door open and stomps inside, adjusting his wide load. His wife pauses with her lipstick-stained teacup halfway to her lips. "You're home early, honey," she says tremulously from her jasmine steam cloud.

"Jig's up," he growls. "Be my whore, or I'll divulge your pen name to the neighbors."

Her hand goes up to the red-rimmed "O" of her lips. She sets down the cup in its saucer with a small clink and drops to her knees. "Of course, whatever you want, honey." She lifts her Save the Manatees sweatshirt to reveal a red lace teddy with nipple cutouts.

"Hello?" Dean snaps in his ear. "Yo, dick brain?"

"Earth to Stud Man," Doug says. "You gonna give us some dirt, or what?"

"Yeah, your mind's definitely in the gutter." Dave orders another round. "Should've seen the look on your face."

"Well, you know, it's private. Husband and wife."

"Yeah, and the thirty thousand people who read her stories!"

He can't blame his wife for his current status as a begrudging icon of virility. She would have kept her kinky stories a secret, but he blurted out the news to the world when the *Penthouse* check arrived. He hadn't considered the ramifications. Well, maybe he had, just a little. He was not without pride at his own magnanimity in allowing her to be who she was. That he didn't hold his wife's rampant public perversions in check, but allowed them to march unfettered across magazine racks far and wide, was a testament to his part in Steinem's new race of unthreatened Man. What other husband would be so secure in his manhood that he would be permissive—nay, *encouraging*—of his wife's transgressive acts, particularly when they did not involve his own penis? Involved a whole parade of phantom penises, in point of fact.

Ironically, from what he's heard, his neighborhood has an above average *times-per-week* compared to most suburban outposts, owing to the fervor of imagination the erotica writer and her husband inspire.

Does he want them to know the truth, or does he want to continue to stand tall among them as the man who is getting the most nookie? The rare beast who has to keep up with his wife's ravenous appetite? The stallion who snagged a nymphomaniac? The man who has the pleasure of acting out every filthy scenario she devises? He has more sexual intrigue than the guys on covers of romance novels. He's not mowing the lawn like the rest of these poor schmucks; he's munching her bush.

"It's fiction," he finally ventures to his bar mates in response. "You don't have to commit murder to write a mystery."

They snort and pump their hips suggestively. A woman down the bar looks at them in disgust and carries her Pinot Grigio to a distant table.

Dean notes his scratched wrists. "Whoa! She got a little carried away, huh?"

"So what *is* the little lady up to tonight?" Doug asks.

"She's got a friend coming over."

"You dog!" Dave wipes his beer moustache. "A threesome!"

He bangs the front door open and stomps inside. His wife and her friend pause with their lipstick-stained teacups half way to their lips. "Jig's up," he growls. "Be my sluts, or I'll delete your American Idols *off the TiVo."*

Her hand goes up to the red-rimmed "O" of her lips. She sets down the cup in its saucer with a small clink and drops to her knees. "Of course, whatever you want, honey. You, too, right, Becky?" His wife lifts her orange knit poncho to reveal a black leather bustier with nipple cutouts. But Becky, being small, quick, and lithe, has already crawled halfway across the floor, on a mission to get his cock into her mouth before his wife can. Her breasts fall out of her cardigan as she makes like a Slinky towards him, saying, "I've been hungry for you to ask me! All of my sinful stories are just flimsy coverups for the real fantasies I'm having about you! Come to mama, my divine sausage, and gimme the works."

"It's a dirty job, but somebody's gotta do it."

When he leaves awhile later, whistles and catcalls follow him out the door into the rainy night.

He pulls into the driveway of 613 Cedar Lane and surveys the dark house. He takes his shoes off on the front porch and carries them inside, careful in his socked feet to make no noise on the wood floor. She's a light sleeper, and the smallest creak that jars her from REM will disrupt her circadian rhythm for weeks.

He hears a small voice calling to him, and he cracks open the bedroom door. His wife sits propped up in the bed, in a dim circle of light from her bed lamp, sudoku book and pencil in hand. A teacup and saucer perch on the comforter beside her.

"Glad you're home," she yawns. "You saved me from myself. I was about to cheat. How pathetic."

"What're you doing still up? Thought you had to get back to work at the crack of dawn."

"Couldn't sleep. Missed you." She pats the bed beside her.

"Hold on a sec." He holds up the buttermilk. "Lemme put this away first."

"Nuke this for me while you're up?" She holds out the teacup.

He punches in 22 seconds on the microwave. There's not a lot he feels he can do for her, other than the occasional oil change or too-tight jar lid. But if she's comfy on the couch and in the middle of a book, she can, without a word, hold out her half-finished tea to him on his way past. He's got it down to a science and punches in numbers on the timer depending on how empty the cup is. She likes her tea hot, but not too hot.

He hands her the warmed cup and stretches out beside her. She wrinkles her nose while she sips.

"Too hot?" Impossible.

"No. It's just that it's chamomile."

"I thought you hated chamomile."

"I do. It's so horsy-smelling. I feel like I'm in chewing cud. In a barn. In Kentucky. But it's supposed to be good for you. Helps with dewey skin or better eyesight or memory or something. I'm old and fat. I need all the help I can get. Can't hurt. Think I should cover my gray?"

Uh oh, bad writing day, he can tell. "What gray?"

"I don't believe you, but thanks, hon. What'd you and the boys talk about tonight?"

"That crabbing show. They filmed the last episode at the same bar we were at."

"That *Deadliest Crabs* one?"

"No, I had those once, and it's nothing you'd care to film."

She laughs. "What else?"

"Just the game and stuff."

She rolls her eyes. "You boys have no imagination."

He bangs the front door open and stomps inside. Naked, his wife sits backwards on his favorite armchair, her breasts pressed to the chair back. Her legs are spread side, and the crack of her ass holds communion with the seat. Tattoos of naked women cover her back. "Oh, honey," she looks at him over her shoulder. "Look what I got done today. I was out shopping for pumps, you know with the arch support like I need? Which reminds me, I need to take my glucosamine later. Anyway, I just felt like something a little more fun, y'know? Some good ole retail therapy. The grind's really getting to me lately. I started with stilettos, and wound up with ink, and a nipple and a guiche piercing, too. I just figured, why not go the whole nine yards? Come see." She swivels around and slouches low in the chair, hooking her legs up over the arms to give him a full display. *"Slather some ointment on me, and then fuck me up the ass, hard as you can, 'kay? And tomorrow we'll get you something fun, too. Maybe a cock ring. Although,"* she muses, *"it might be tough to find one big enough for you. Maybe special order?"*

"You don't think so, huh?"

She snaps the book shut. "Try me."

"What've you got on under that nightie?" Tonight it's the daisy-print flannel. The nursing one she bought by mistake, with lots of convenient buttons that she starts to undo.

"Guess, Mr. Cocky Brainstorm."

"Nothing."

"Bingo."

"My favorite."

"What'd you boys *really* talk about? Were they at it again? All with anal sex on their mind but too afraid to ask about it? Like it makes them pansies or something?"

She still wants to talk. He's in no hurry. It's one of those things all those sex movies fail to mention: the small talk. He shifts closer towards her. He knows what this is, these superficial questions of hers. To someone else it might seem like idle chitchat, meaningless dithering going nowhere. But he recognizes it for what it is: foreplay. Getting reacquainted again after the daily separations of a humdrum life. A casual reconnection before the more intimate one that he knows is around the next bend. Step on the gas and try to cut a corner and it's all over before it started. She'll cut the engine.

"They think I'm having a threesome."

She looks around the room. "There's always the cat."

"That's not the pussy I had in mind."

"No?"

His hand creeps up under her nightie, finds her inner thigh, and he lets it rest there, just shy of his ultimate target. Her hand simultaneously finds his fly, and she starts undoing the buttons with one hand. All that typing has at least helped keep her fingers strong.

"I was thinking," he says, his hands just brushing the tips of her pubic hair. "Maybe I'll write a story."

"Oh, sure, everyone thinks it's easy. But try coming up with new ideas all the time."

"Yeah," he says, his finger finding the bull's-eye, "that must be tough."

My Wife Taste Tests Her Chocolates

My wife taste tests her chocolates,
presents half-eaten remainders to me.
Gnawed fudge neat in accordion cup, or
nipped bonbon in re-twisted foil wrapper,
or a white bar with one corner missing,
dog-eared reminder of her dislikes.
One bite enough to know no good.
Oozy filling, or too bitter, or
the shock of a concealed, congealed cherry.
Choosy, she assesses with surreptitious lips, a
mouse nibbling the mousse.

She bestows tampered treats like a hand-crafted gift,
teeth marks carved into smooth artist's clay.
For you! her notes say, as if these
traumatized leftovers cost her dearly,
surpassing the price of surprise plane tickets to Paris, a
wrenching sacrifice to desert them.

She knows their worth,
no trifles, these marooned macaroons.
Shared rejects surpass kiss's intimacy.
This truffle nested atop her tongue, a
wedding ring on a pillow.
She opened herself to this candy.

She would offer this sugared scrap to no one
but me.
There is nothing she would not give me, this
chewed confection declares.
She will never discard me.

Cellophane crinkles as I undress her
tender. I lay her wafer in my mouth.
With this blessed dessert, I thee swallow.
I take her in, the other half of me, as
her body so often receives mine when
we are wrapped in bed sheets.
Honeyed detritus melts me, inside me.
I savor her sweet gesture,
melded so we can no more tell
who the hard caramel center,
and who the cocoa butter embrace.

About the Author

Jennifer D. Munro grew up in Hawaii as a fourth-generation islander and now lives in the Pacific Northwest. Her stories and essays have appeared in numerous literary journals and anthologies, including The Bigger the Better the Tighter the Sweater: 21 Funny Women on Beauty and Body Image; Best American Erotica; Best Women's Erotica; Mammoth Book of Best New Erotica; Literary Mama; North American Review; Secrets & Confidences: The Complicated Truth About Women's Friendships; They Lied: True Tales of Pregnancy; Tarnished: True Tales of Innocence Lost; Brain, Child: The Magazine for Thinking Mothers; Thou Shalt Not: Stories of Dark Crime and Horror; & Zyzzyva.
She blogs about marriage, miscarriage, motorcycling, and motherhood at www.StraightNoChaserMom.com.
Website: www.munrojd.com.

Acknowledgements

Thanks to the following:

Jackson, Meredith, and Maureen, first and best readers, and amazing friends. I couldn't do it without you.
Tod for computer & website assistance, for prodding me to get my work out of drawers, but most of all for friendship.
Leslie & Scot for their love, support, and cold hard cash.
Dr. Munro and Maureen for grammar and editing expertise.
Bob for creative brainstorming and for an eventual book cover.
Hedgebrook for time in paradise.
Artist Trust Grants for Artist Projects for much-needed funds.
Joel Chafetz, Lisa Schlesinger, Redmond Association of Spoken Word, and Seattle Writers Association for early encouragement.
Jesse, Rachel & John, Mary, Irene, Jenny, Marjorie, Skye, and all the writers in my life who have encouraged me.
The England-Markuns for sharing good times in Mexico.
Mr. Hopps, for coaching me through my first public reading.
The editors who have improved and published my work.
Ricardo, for everything you put up with. Damn, you're still hot.